SACRAMENTO PUBLIC LIBRARY
828 "I" Street
Sacramento, CA 958

Praise for Kristín Eiríksdóttir

2013: Nominated for the Icelandic Women's Literature Prize for *Hvítfeld – fjölskyldusaga* (*White Fur: Story of a Family*)

2014: Winner of the Icelandic Bookseller's Prize for *KOK* (*Throat*, a poetry collection)

2014: Nominated for the Icelandic Literary Prize for *KOK* (*Throat*)

2015: Nominated for the DV Cultural Prize for Drama for *Hystory*

"Truly one of the most remarkable works of fiction this year by a young and fantastic writer."

—*Fréttatíminn* weekly about *Doris Dies*

"In her first novel, Eiríksdóttir displays a rare mastery of the form—it would be surprising if this were not the beginning of the career of a spectacular novelist."

—*Fréttablaðið* about *White Fur*

"Kristín Eiríksdóttir is one of our finest young writers . . . she has a completely unique vision."

—Egill Helgason, *Kiljan*, Icelandic National Television

Praise for *A Fist or a Heart*

2017: Winner of the Icelandic Literary Prize

2017: Icelandic Bookseller's Prize second place

2017: Icelandic National Broadcasting Service's best novels of 2017

2018: Winner of the Icelandic Women's Literature Prize

2018: Nominated for the DV Cultural Prize

2019: Nominated for the Nordic Council Literature Prize

"A finely wrought and extremely detailed novel. Excellent stuff."

—Auður Jónsdóttir, award-winning author

"A particularly sensitive and affecting exploration of the way people sense reality, of the mind's escape routes, of loneliness, the forgotten, and the hidden. The narrative technique is at once thoughtful and effortless, which reflects both the characters and subject matter. In keeping with the book's leitmotif, the author creates imagery that appeals to all of the senses, and she uses (among other things) powerful signs that are still never obvious or superficial. [*A Fist or a Heart*] is an extremely well-written novel that lives on with the reader."

—Jury of the Icelandic Women's Literature Prize

"Her work is entirely different than that of other authors . . . She is extremely clever in the way she constructs narrative, navigates the fictional world, creates characters, and begins her narrative thread in an understated way, then intensifies exponentially . . . Impressive and especially moving . . . she is especially skilled at playing with her audience's heart—the way she creates a narrative climax that eludes every one of the reader's defenses, directly piercing the vulnerable heart and remaining long after the reader has finished the book . . . Kristín Eiríksdóttir is simply the most interesting Icelandic author today!"

—Vera Knútsdóttir, Bokmenntaborgin.is, website of the Reykjavík UNESCO City of Literature office

"In a sensitive and beautiful way, [*A Fist or a Heart*] discusses people and their personal quirks—people who may also have darker stories to tell than might first seem evident. Kristín Eiríksdóttir has a special talent for communicating the sensory through text, everything from the smallest and most fragile to the huge and grotesque."

—Guðrún Baldvinsdóttir, Icelandic National Broadcasting Service

"This book is much greater than its number of pages suggests . . . You could read and reread the book again and again and let the narrative themes wind themselves together in completely new ways."

—Sunna Dís Másdóttir, *Kiljan*, Icelandic National Television

"Kristín Eiríksdóttir is a very special author . . . I wanted to read the book again immediately after finishing it . . . She's able to screw with your mind . . . Sometimes you doubt whether you should allow her into your head, because she will turn everything upside down . . . This book's development affected me so much that when I looked up from it, I felt I wasn't seeing the world through the right eyes . . . Kristín Eiríksdóttir is simply my favorite author under forty . . . Her writing is so exciting, especially in the way the narrative threads connect to her other works."

—Haukur Ingvarsson, *Kiljan*, Icelandic National Television

"[*A Fist or a Heart*] is spun from countless threads that branch out widely, but that in the end form a strong whole . . . Ellen and Elín— these contrasting women—have much in common: They are lonely and exceptional in their fields, and both were raised in poor circumstances by women who were not entirely there. Both are fatherless . . . Yet another important thread is memory and forgetfulness, a theme that is entwined to an extent with the narrative itself—Elín tells the story, but she is not completely reliable. When she tells Ellen's story the reader doesn't know what is 'true' and what is improvised, based on gossip or imagination. At the end, her memory betrays her and the logical context of existence becomes confused—she loses control of her life and the story slips from her grip . . . Eiríksdóttir has a unique and personal style that is both challenging and charming . . . Little by little, a picture is drawn for the reader of a story full of pain, loneliness, and dramatic events."

—Hildigunnur Þráinsdóttir, *Morgunblaðið* (Reykjavík)

"This is a book that one simply needs to read again, and perhaps again. It is always satisfying when a novel hits hard, or weaves a spell like this one, leaving behind uncertainty."

—Ingi Freyr Vilhjálmsson, *Stundin* (Reykjavík)

A FIST

OR A

HEART

A FIST
OR A
HEART

KRISTÍN EIRÍKSDÓTTIR

Translated by LARISSA KYZER

amazoncrossing

This is a work of fiction. Names, characters, organizations, places, events, and incidents are either products of the author's imagination or are used fictitiously. Any resemblance to actual persons, living or dead, or actual events is purely coincidental.

Text copyright © 2017 by Kristín Eiríksdóttir
Translation copyright © 2019 by Larissa Kyzer

All rights reserved.

No part of this book may be reproduced, or stored in a retrieval system, or transmitted in any form or by any means, electronic, mechanical, photocopying, recording, or otherwise, without express written permission of the publisher.

Previously published as *Elín, ýmislegt* by Forlagid, www.forlagid.is, in Iceland in 2017. Translated from Icelandic by Larissa Kyzer. First published in English by AmazonCrossing in 2019.

Published by AmazonCrossing, Seattle

www.apub.com

Amazon, the Amazon logo, and AmazonCrossing are trademarks of Amazon.com, Inc., or its affiliates.

ISBN-13: 9781542044035 (hardcover)
ISBN-10: 1542044030 (hardcover)
ISBN-13: 9781542044028 (paperback)
ISBN-10: 1542044022 (paperback)

Cover design by Joan Wong

Printed in the United States of America

First edition

A FIST
OR A
HEART

My hands get no cleaner than an old bathtub. My fingernails are all clipped as short as possible, but the chemicals have managed to claw their way through the dead skin, into the bone. As if there's no enamel.

When I say *bone*, I mean the nails, because nails are a kind of bone. Or rather, *horn* would maybe be a better word, but at any rate, it's as if some chemicals have blended with the proteins that weave the nails together. When I say *dead skin*, I just mean the outermost layer of the skin. It's just dead cells.

Then under it, there's the dermis, and under the dermis is the hypodermis.

Life.

My hands look dirty. But in reality, they're clean. They're cracked from hand washing and the cold. Coarse from use. Large and thick because that's how hands are in my family. The legs in my family are short. So we don't have to bend too far down to the dirt. And our toes are squat. The soles of our feet are flat under the weight of the temperaments we carry on these short legs. In these large, outstretched hands.

My name is Elín Jónsdóttir. Daughter of Guðrún and Jón. Birth year, 1946. Birthday, the ninth of January. They're deceased, Guðrún and Jón. Have been for some time. I'm mother to no one.

I make props, but I'm no novelist. Though there're probably some similarities between these two crafts, there are, nevertheless, many more differences. In order to write this, I have to sit still and use my hands in such a way that my back is becoming riddled with pain.

I don't know how to touch-type and use only the index finger on my left hand and the middle and ring fingers on my right. I alternate staring down at the keyboard and up at the screen and then something happens. My mind wanders from the material, leaves the pain behind, teeters on the rooftop.

The reason I decided to write this is that if I don't, no one will—a predictable outcome. The injustice of the story is, nevertheless, a matter of no importance; there's injustice because injustice is everywhere. Intrinsic to our stories because it's intrinsic to us.

When I say *us*, I feel as though I'm lying. Maybe if I say it more often. Over and over again.

Then would I start to believe that it's true?

US.

I'll say it just to absolve myself of responsibility—I'm talking about myself, but I'm trying to drag you all through the mud with me. The injustice is *here*, within me, which is why I'm dwelling on it—not on you.

YOU.

My respect for YOU has been shattered countless times, disintegrated many times over, and disappears and reappears and is smashed into pieces. Every diagnosis contains a hundred, and all of them are wrong. All of them are right. Nothing you do is wrong. Everything you do is terrifying.

And there's a good reason why no one would write this story: Because there is no story. Just an attempt to connect signs that were conveyed in waking life and in dreams. Don't worry—I'm not going to lull you to sleep with dreams—but the signs make it clear to me that the brain is not something you can touch.

The same is true for all things, and that's what this story is about.

But not about a girl.

Whose name is Ellen.

I met her the day after the boxes were found. Which is so typical of this whole story that it all flows together in my mind. Ellen flows up out of and down into the boxes—lost, found, stolen cardboard boxes.

Not long before, whiteflies had shown up, yet again. I'd already tried all sorts of things—vinegar, dishwashing liquid. All that stuff. Separated the plants, sprayed them, dried them out. The flies always came back until at last, I gave up and threw the plants out.

It was rough. They were all from people I cared about, most of whom were dead. I'm not saying, mind you, that I was *devastated*, or that I'd *cried*. But it was very trying all the same.

A week later, something happened that I also associate with Ellen Álfsdóttir and the three boxes:

I was messing around with the cords behind the television—an old tube TV connected to an antenna, the old-fashioned way—when I closed my hand around a living thing. In a manner of speaking, cords are, of course, living things. Or anyway, the electricity that travels through them isn't *dead*, but the thing I was touching was different. It was organic. I was stooped over a dark corner and felt its vital signs and tugged.

It was a plant. Not one of the plants I'd thrown out. It was unlike any plant I'd seen before, in the sense that it had no roots, no bottom. A perfectly self-sustaining tangle that drew breath. Like some David Attenborough program had taken a shit behind the television.

Tillandsia, said the internet. A plant from Central and South America. A rootless plant that lives on air. Bright green leaves, long and delicate, that grow in a strangely symmetrical fashion, as if each leaf was trying to envelop the next. Like some kind of orgy, and I peered into it, searching for something that might be the beginning or the middle, but I found nothing.

Some types grow flowers, I read, and indeed, I saw signs of this on my plant. A minuscule pink bud in one spot.

Logical readers might imagine that some friend of mine must have wanted to have a bit of fun and surprise me with this fanciful gift, which gives me the chance to insert something important, namely:

I don't have any friends. Not a single one.

No one's crazy. I mean what I say. There are so many sides to reality that, in the best-case scenario, it's cubistic. Worst-case scenario, predictable. Never flat.

A week later, the real estate agent called and told me that they'd found a cold little storage room in my grandma's old house that wasn't on any of the blueprints, and that in it, there were three boxes with my name on them.

It was odd. I had never considered what had become of my belongings from my childhood and teenage years. It was like I assumed they'd just vanished of their own volition. Some things I'd thrown out; other things were lost. The rest had maybe gotten mixed in with someone else's stuff, or had left home, like me.

But there were three boxes, said the real estate agent. Boxes that someone must have specially sorted.

ELÍN, PAPERS
ELÍN, BOOKS
ELÍN, MISC.

All the worldly belongings I'd left behind in my bedroom all those years ago.

In addition to those three boxes, there were a few boxes of books in the storage room, a pile of tablecloths and embroidery, broken audio equipment, dust, mouse droppings, and spiderwebs.

I'd tried to avoid everything concerning that apartment—just hired a property manager and paid the bills—and now it was empty, spotlessly white with a gleaming floor, and pictures of it had run in the newspaper's real estate pages. Everything was ready when this storage unit in the basement came to light.

I don't even have a broom, I apologized after we'd stacked the boxes in the back seat of my car. The real estate agent waved that away, said she'd take care of it. She was on edge. As if she were selling her first property or wasn't a real estate agent at all. Young and fast-talking, as if she were performing the idea of a man.

Thank you, I said, leaving her with the spiderwebs and mouse droppings. I asked her to take the embroidery to the local charity shop, and I knew very well that I was belittling her, but that was okay, wasn't it?

Maybe I even enjoyed it a little.

We all have our quirks.

On my way home, I listened to the news on the radio. Police were seeking information on the whereabouts of a pale man, wearing a parka and gloves. It was the beginning of February and dark. I wondered who wouldn't be pale and wearing a parka and gloves right now.

Back at home, Ellen's script was waiting for me, unread. The script for the play that would be staged in the fall. Rumor had it that it was completely finished, that its construction was perfect, and that if the director tried to change so much as a comma, the whole thing would go to pieces. By all accounts, its characterization was unprecedentedly vivid, its style exceptional.

I flipped straight to the character descriptions and squinted at the page:

THE FATHER:
A splotch of bandages, some of them sodden. Yet nothing
is wrong.

It had been a long time since I'd gone near a theater. When I was younger, I sometimes worked in the prop department for short periods of time, but for the last thirty years, I'd really only worked in film and television.

Hreiðar, the director who was going to stage the young genius's play, had mostly made movies, even though like me, he'd gotten his start in the theater. I'd worked with him often. Now he was middle-aged and had been known as the Next Big Thing for the past twenty years. Which is to say that the theater had the idea to bring him in for this play, and he was probably desperate. Wanted to have a hit—a shark in formaldehyde—something that freed him of people's expectations and guaranteed him some security.

Oh, security!

When he'd called and asked if I had time, my first reaction was to say no. Mainly because I'd become so consumed with close-ups, minutiae, perfection. With materials that were like skin. With nuances. With this kind of hyperdelicacy. The degree of concentration that this precision demanded was addictive. In the theater, everyone could care less about that. Movements needed to be large enough that the people in the very back could see them, as did the costumes. The props badly painted Styrofoam and particle board, if I recalled correctly.

Just read the script, said Hreiðar. You're going to love the descriptions. It's perfect for a modernist like you—we've just got to have you on the team. You're gonna love it.

I promise, he said, and I was going to say goodbye when he dropped the young genius's name.

Ellen Álfsdóttir, he said.

Álfur Finnsson's daughter? I asked.

Yes, that's right, he said. Quite a selling point. We've got the big stage, plenty of money—that's why I'm calling you.

Is the first read-through this coming Monday?

Do you want to join us? he asked, clearly unprepared for me to say yes. The first reading's on Monday, he then hurried to say. Naturally, you don't have to come to the rehearsal unless you want to . . . but of course you're very welcome.

Send me the play, I said, and in almost the same moment, I received a new email. I printed the script right away, but since then, it had wandered, unread, between the kitchen table and the living room couch.

I was overcome with the fatigue particular to the short days of winter and got to my feet, went into the living room. Everything was a mess. My work space was constantly eating up square footage in the house. There were many pounds of clay underneath a thick plastic sheet on the dining table. Curving up out of the middle of the clay and sticking through a hole cut in the plastic was a horn that I was shaping. The horn was supposed to look like a rhinoceros horn that played a big part in a movie that was to be shot over the summer, but the director didn't want to use a real horn, for political reasons.

The world hungered for young geniuses. I'd watched a few of them meet with success and then disappear altogether, or else fall in line with other unexciting working bards. As a rule, it wasn't their genius that captivated people, but rather just their freshness and youth. Their skin, not their talent. The hope for something new draped like an invisible cloak over the stale old lore that men had gone on reciting, over and over and over.

Ellen's father, Álfur Finnsson, had also been the Next Big Thing in his time, and later, a distinguished author. He died many years ago. He was a playwright, among other things, and I'd actually worked on a few of his productions. Gotten to know him a little.

Back around 1980, I built a mountain out of sod that was blown up during every performance as soon as the curtain was raised, night after night. The duration of his life was as tragic and dramatic as his writings. Not least the end of it, and Ellen was only maybe two years old then.

My interest in her play undoubtedly stemmed from this as well. A lot had been written about Álfur Finnsson and his work, but very little was actually known about his final years. About the young woman with whom he had a daughter, Ellen.

He was five or so years older than me, and I remember all too well the hubbub that his first book generated. Later, when I'd started to work a little at the theater, and we met, I was rather intrigued by him. Not so much that I wanted to get to know him, though, and I never admired him. But it isn't often that you meet people who have such an easy time of manipulating their surroundings and filling them with salacious stories.

I followed the gossip about him, listened from a distance. It was like every other soap opera, of course, and how was any of that my business?

Until I accidentally got mixed up in the most salacious story of them all.

I found my reading glasses next to the TV remote and then went back into the kitchen and sat down to read again, but I couldn't stay focused. When I'd looked up rhinos online a few days earlier, countless close-ups of wounds had come up and ever since, I hadn't been able to stop thinking about this act: *ripping a horn off a rhino's face.*

Afterward, the horns were sold on the black market.

No, I had to finish the horn. Then I could read the girl's master-piece. I wrapped my work shirt around me and turned on the radio, sat down at the table, and carved very fine lines into the clay with a bristly wire brush.

My grandma died almost forty years ago. I threw out everything without remembering that I'd done it. Sometimes, I doubt that's true, but it must be. Who else would have done it?

No, it must have been me, in shock, racked with guilt as I filled trash bags with my grandma's life and shuttled them to the dump.

I imagined that my hands belonged to someone else. Everything had to go to the dump. Everything reminded me of disease and despair. Even those objects saturated with memories of better times became depressing in this context—so depressing that they had to go to the dump.

When I looked at my hands in front of me, it was like they belonged to someone else who was sawing infected limbs from an otherwise healthy torso. If there was to be any kind of hope for me, it all had to go to the dump.

I have a hazy recollection of cleaning the apartment. I was twenty-seven years old, an entirely different woman, crawling around and scrubbing on all fours, and the next thing I remember is the family that rented the apartment. The first tenants. They were lovely and lived in Grandma's apartment for many years.

When they moved out and I went over to prepare for the next tenants, everything was different. A strange, new grief had intermingled with the old.

There was always an aura of tragedy in that apartment, and it just got worse with every new round of tenants.

I worked in the prop department of a theater where my grandma had arranged a job for me many years before, and I didn't know how I'd get over the shock.

An old coworker of my grandma's told me to go to art school. She mentioned the sculpture program at the Royal Danish Academy. Then she helped me with the application. I didn't even have a high school diploma, but somehow I got in.

Over the next few years, I lived and studied in Copenhagen. It never occurred to me that I was an artist, but I learned much that would come in handy in my work. Learned about colors, shapes, forms, and materials.

Okay, maybe it occurred to me. I'd only say it in a whisper. It occurred to me while I was working on my final project, casting a statue of Heracles and clawing at it with the point of a needle until nothing was left but a mound of chalk.

When I came home in 1980, I bought my house. A hundred-year-old sheep shed that had long ago been converted into residential housing, was then relinquished, then reclaimed, then relinquished, then reclaimed once more. An outbuilding in downtown Reykjavík they'd forgotten to tear down.

I took out a mortgage on Grandma's apartment to buy the house. The owner was an old man who'd been renting it out. The tenants were roughly my own age. They told me it was beset by sick-building syndrome, ghosts, mold in the bathroom. She was pregnant and they were happy to move; this wasn't what they wanted for their baby.

There was a crawl space in the stone foundation, damp and moldy. Under that, there was a sewage pipe that had long since rusted through, and so the house was standing in shit.

I moved into a cheap guesthouse in the area and took my time renovating the foundation—exterminating, lifting, rebuilding, putting in a sewage pipe, learning all about dampness and ventilation. Adjusted the conditions, changed materials. Rebuilt. Took out a second mortgage.

The lumber was rotten in some places, but I wanted to keep the original wood, soft pine that had lapped up the house's whole history and quietly stored it away. After I'd rooted out the cause of the damp, I removed each plank, evaluated its condition, and dried and warmed it before nailing it back in place or changing it out for a new one.

I also deepened the cellar, since I was down there with a shovel anyway. That's where I kept my tools and materials and during my most toxic, most squalid projects, I stayed down there, too. It has four windows that can be cracked to allow neighborhood cats to wander in, but I also installed a powerful ventilation system and fan.

My living room and the kitchen are on the ground floor. Each with its own space. It's hard for me to understand this mania people have for open plans. Having a kitchen in the living room seems like just as good an idea as having the toilet in there. Behind a sliding French door at the far end of the living room there's a work room, and next to that, there's a small bedroom.

I sleep on a hard chaise lounge because it's better for my back and because when I sleep, I always lie absolutely still, always wake in the same position I fell asleep in. Like a fox in its burrow.

But I'm thankful for my house.

Every nail is right where I put it.

If the paneling swells, I've only myself to blame.

I know exactly where the plumbing is.

There's a loft in the attic. Sometime around 2000, I raised the roof and put in a splendid dormer made from fragrant, freshly cut wood. At the same time, I installed a studio apartment in the attic that I now rent under the table.

The woman who rents from me is a single mother. Her name is Helen and her kid is with her every other week. Then I hear quick footsteps and the odd burst of tears. On alternate weeks, she's not at home much. She probably has a lover whom she stays with.

When I drove to the theater to attend the first table reading, the script sat unread on the passenger seat. The night before, I'd gotten distracted trying to get the right texture in the clay, and before I knew it, it had gotten so late that it was time to go to bed.

The cast had gathered in a meeting room along with the director, set designer, and playwright. The way it usually worked was that they read over the play slowly and carefully, considering the significance of this or that scene.

This was one of the dullest things I could think of doing. There were always one or two people in the group who'd latch on to a word and hold it hostage. Who'd drone and whisper about anonymous individuals whose names they'd then blurt out. And before you knew it, the discussion would have gotten way off track and be headed still further afield. All depending on how good the director was at their job, that is.

Even though I was a little late, I grabbed myself a cup of coffee before strolling into the meeting room. They were all there. The actors, with their open, enthusiastic faces; the smartly dressed set designer; the director, all his flaws and affectations completely unchecked; and, at the end of the table, the playwright.

Ellen looked like she was not yet twenty. She sat with her head bowed, her greasy, shiny black hair hiding half her face, and her buttermilk skin immediately catching my attention. I wanted to sit close to her so I could get a better look and grabbed a folding chair that I more or less crammed in between her and the actors. The director introduced me to the group.

Elín'll be capturing the father, the bandage heap, he said boorishly and smirked.

And the "slush machine" in the second act, said the set designer, making air quotes and smiling flirtatiously at the playwright.

When I'd gotten closer, I realized that her skin wasn't actually the color of buttermilk. Rather, it was the lightest shade of lime green—one shade darker than white—which is why she seemed luminescent. What was, nevertheless, most peculiar about this skin of hers was how thick and supple it was. Her pores were so small as to be invisible.

Her skin was so thick that you couldn't see her veins anywhere; her skin was the exact same pale white–lime green all over. Like a cheap doll. If I had to make a wax figure of Ellen Álfsdóttir, she'd look artificial.

Unlike the rest of her visible hair, Ellen's eyelashes were white, which muted her whole appearance. How odd, I thought. I peered at her scalp to check whether her hair was colored and immediately saw the fresh shadow of hair dye. Two showers would take it out completely, but a few inches of white roots were already on display.

She was wearing a white T-shirt that looked dirty, although in all likelihood, it had just been washed so much that it was starting to pill. With the shirt, she'd paired shiny sweatpants that buttoned down the sides, white gym socks with blue and red stripes, and black patent-leather shoes.

Like a vagrant.

I'd noticed this trend and was puzzled by it. All these young, attractive people who slouched around in rags that'd been bought at some co-op in the '90s and then worn by a goose farmer for years on end, sold at the Red Cross charity shop, and were now recontextualized by youth and beauty. If I dressed like Ellen Álfsdóttir, I'd be dismissed as a bag lady on sight.

I glanced around for a sweater or jacket, but saw nothing that might belong to her except for a crumpled, tacky acrylic sweater over in the corner. Who throws their sweater on the floor during their first meeting in a new workplace? I thought, feeling unexpectedly concerned for the young playwright.

I pictured her mother, exhausted, tidying up as she went, always complaining and full of self-pity, while simultaneously neglecting to teach her child how to behave at the most basic level.

I wonder how her mother's doing?

So, the slush machine is actually some kind of mouth? brayed the set designer. She directed the question at Ellen, who up until that point, hadn't said a single word. I looked at her expectantly, waiting for her complexion to change, for her cheeks to redden or whiten, but nothing changed. She directed her stone-gray eyes at the set designer and answered.

Mouth or semen slit or asshole, it doesn't really matter, she said, and everyone laughed. Maybe she's more confident than she looks, I thought, but then she got a puzzled expression on her face. She was surprised.

When I got home, I saw the boxes on the living room floor and decided to take them to the recycling center. I've no need for mysterious time capsules in my life, I thought, and felt relieved.

I carried the boxes out to the car, drove out to the drop-off point in the half-light, listened to the news on the radio. They were still searching for the pale man wearing a parka and gloves. I drove up the ramp with shipping containers on either side, but when I reached the one for nonrecyclable waste, I remembered something.

A golden journal with angels on the front. They were deep in thought, their hands under their chins. Grandma gave me that journal.

I didn't stop the car, but instead kept driving past all the shipping containers and back downtown. I stopped at a Thai restaurant, ordered pad thai, and took it home with me to eat while I watched the news.

The boxes were back on my living room floor.

ELÍN, MISC.

That night, I cast the rhino horn and got started preparing for my next project with the same director. The burned body parts of a teenage girl. I read medical reports about fire-related deaths and did a horrific image search online.

The film director asked me to bring the rhino horn to his house. I told him that wasn't going to work for me, but he could pick up the horn whenever he liked. Then he said he needed to run something by me, which made me curious, and I said I'd drop by.

This was his first full-length film and the first time I'd worked for him. I'd read the script and thought it was fine—your quintessential Nordic crime flick, maybe, but that was okay. There were a few plot points that bothered me, but I wasn't generally asked my opinion about these things and neither did I feel any particular need to share it.

The movie would be like a little chat, a collective dream preoccupied with the same old fixation, varying levels of guilt in regard to the abuse of a girl-child. Everyone was guilty, but some were more guilty than others. Someone the most guilty, someone else the least guilty. Girl-children were like conjunctions—characterless, and yet the whole basis by which sentences hung together.

He lived in a nice neighborhood, in a large single-family house right next to the sea. He was a lot younger than me—still shy of sixty, perhaps—and had two little kids with a popular actress. We sat by a window that looked out over the ocean. The floor was covered with cardboard to protect it from the encroachment of the decorators. There were a few color swatches hanging on the wall. A few different shades of ochre. He took the rhino horn from me and unwrapped the cloth around it, setting it on the table in between us.

Splendid, he said bemusedly, running his fingers over its scaly surface.

But what is it you want to talk about? I asked, and for a moment, it occurred to me that maybe he was after some advice on his house. That maybe I was supposed to select the right shade of ochre for his living room wall.

He looked at me sheepishly.

The producer is making a bit of a fuss, he said, and I relaxed.

The mother, he went on. He doesn't think the character is believable enough, and the script doctor gave me some suggestions. So I'm working on this character, and we decided to give her a scar, see? On her face. And it occurred to us—occurred to me—that she's around your age . . . and I wondered if I might ask you a few questions about . . . well, what it's like to be you?

His head was an unfortunate shape. Like a button mushroom. A face on a stalk and an interminable forehead—you could hardly see his eyes for that forehead. I suddenly remembered a trip I took many years ago, to Myanmar.

I remembered sitting with an herbalist in his tent. He was wearing a long, patterned skirt, and his chest and arms were covered in tiny bamboo tattoos. He was holding a monkey skull over a pot, scraping it with a bread knife. He was surrounded by elephant tusks and hammered brass and gongs and tortoise shells and mahogany roots and tiger claws. A young woman sat next to him, her forehead and cheeks painted white. Her little boy had colic and wept piteously.

He spoke very fast, and the tour guide translated for me simultaneously. The herbalist told me about his tattoos, by which the natives could identify one another's tribes. He explained that he himself was part of the Mon tribe, as was most of his village. The tour guide was also Mon. I asked about the Konyak people, as I'd read that this tribe had long engaged in head-hunting and that for every head a Konyak man accrued, he received a special tattoo.

The tour guide glowered at me and didn't translate the question. Later, he explained that people didn't just hold forth on the Konyak tribe. He got a secretive look on his face, as he often did, looked around to make sure that no one was listening, and explained that Konyak men had stopped head-hunting for the most part, but that if they saw someone with a really unusual head, it might be hard for some of them to resist the temptation. Then he winked at me.

I looked directly at the film director and thought he might well get into trouble if he ran into the Konyak people on the border of Myanmar and India. I was silent. The silence became increasingly uncomfortable, but that wasn't really my problem.

No, but well, I'm sorry—I know this is absurd . . .

Okay, I said. What do you want to know?

I haven't the slightest idea. Have you ever thought about getting your scar fixed?

I had it fixed as best it could be at the time. Then I got used to it.

Yes, of course, he said, and laughed.

I got to my feet and asked when they planned to shoot.

In the spring, he said. Filming starts in May.

The prop list hasn't changed at all?

No . . . But maybe we'll have you do Astrid's scar?

Sure, I said. I should be able to swing that.

How did she get the scar? I then asked. The director hesitated.
You decide, he said finally. It's never explained in the script.

We said goodbye, and when I was back in the car and reversing
away from the film director's concrete bunker, I saw him standing at the
kitchen window, motionless, his head tilted to one side.

He wanted inside of me. I don't mean sexually. Not at all. But some
people are like that, like this director—can't see anything without wanting to infiltrate it. Ellen's father, Álfur, was like that, too.

I could feel the pressure dropping, a storm gathering. The sky was a monochrome steel gray. I decided to go to the theater where the actors were still stuttering their way through the first of five acts. Ellen sat at the end of the table, apparently distracted, picking at a wart on her index finger.

She was wearing a few wristbands, the kind people get at music festivals. Some of them were old and raggedy, but others were newer. There was a jolt of neon yellow polish on her nails, which had little half-moons of dirt under them.

During the coffee break I went out for a smoke, and Ellen came out a few minutes after me. She greeted me curtly and then got lost in thought, sucking on her cigarette and staring down through the grate I was standing on. Her patent-leather shoes were worn, the skin completely gone over the toes, revealing gray canvas underneath.

Beneath the grate were hundreds of cigarette butts, bleached plastic candy wrappers, crimped beer cans, a debit card. It occurred to me that I should ask her, half-jokingly, if she'd lost her card, but I could see that she was deeply preoccupied.

We stood in silence and I considered the shape of her head. It was normal enough, except at the base, which was a bit flat. Clearly, her mother hadn't turned her enough, I thought as she looked at me coldly.

What? she asked, and I jumped. I froze, said nothing. Just flicked my cigarette down through the grate and went back into the meeting room.

God, she's a genius, the set designer blathered, and everyone murmured their assent. The director said that there hadn't been a debut work of its like in decades.

And so young, said the oldest actor present, shaking his head. It reminds me of Pinter's first play, he added.

First? snorted the next-oldest actor. It's got much more in common with his final works, if I do say so myself. Pinter's early plays were so tedious . . .

Tedious? the oldest asked but didn't take the bait.

Yes, said the next oldest. So poetical it gives you a headache! This play is so well structured, so logical.

There are four characters in the play.

THE GRANDSON (18):
Tinge of royal blue. Tiny braids that move of their own accord. Tiresome nudity. Stale odor of masturbation.

THE SON (42):
Shimmering indigo. Driven by the lower chakra. Perpetually clenched and careful to keep a good grip on the very slippery little pearl that's stuck up his anus at all times.

THE UNCLE (65):
No focal point. A swirl of suede fringe. Shades. Internal disease.

THE FATHER (70):
His eyes are very small, slippery pearls that he must be
careful not to roll right out of his sockets—or worse, back
into his sockets and out through his nostrils. He's accom-
panied by a staid group of fans.

I'm picturing a very raw stage, said the set designer earnestly.

Not a black floor, said the director. And for the love of god, have the actors wear shoes.

If we install a floor, our whole budget will go to that.

Just figure it out. I don't care if you cover it with plastic bags, just not that black chalkboard—I'm so tired of it.

I'm picturing everyone in gray . . .

Not gray, make it . . . and not white or black, either. It doesn't cost anything to color coordinate, am I right? Where's the girl? Wasn't she coming back after the break? When can we get started?

She's probably left, said the youngest actor. I ran into her out front, and that's what it looked like she was doing.

Left? repeated the director. But we're not done—there are still two hours to go.

Psh. Like we said—she's a genuine genius, said the oldest actor.

Brilliance has nothing to do with a poor work ethic, said the next oldest.

Of course it does, said the oldest. When the muse calls, sometimes you just gotta go. It calls and you go!

The next oldest waved this away. I slipped out, no need to say goodbye.

Ellen was walking along the Miklabraut thoroughfare in a gray hood that stuck out from under the collar of her knitted sweater. Her head was drooped, and she moved sluggishly, dragging her feet on the sidewalk.

She's got to be cold, I thought, remembering her patent-leather shoes, imagining that they'd have soaked through almost immediately, that her gym socks were gray from wetness, her toes cold. I pulled the car alongside her at the next light, pushed open the passenger-side door and called to her, asked if she'd like a ride.

But the playwright just looked at me grumpily; the red light gave way to green, and people started honking at me.

I'll drop you at home! I repeated, but Ellen just shook her head, lifted one of her hands, held out her palm with some sloppy scrawl on it that I couldn't read.

Have it your way, then, you little freak, I muttered, and drove off.

She couldn't feel her feet. Like there were ice cubes in her shoes, and each time she took a step, it felt weird, like she was going to collapse. She'd be home soon.

Why were her feet so cold?

Because she didn't have a driver's license.
   Why didn't she have a driver's license?
   Because she didn't have a dad.

Why were her feet so cold?

Her mom could have suggested driving lessons when Ellen was seventeen, but she forgot. Forgot the needs of other people, and her own, and everything.

Why were her feet so cold?

It was something someone said. At the table reading. Said something about something that Ellen had written that hit too close to home. It was unreal. Like the voices in her head had started to distinguish themselves from one another, like a bullet had been shot into a bullet, and she'd had enough. Decided to walk home.

That something that someone said. She remembered it word for word. It had been the next-oldest actor, the one playing the uncle. He was talking about the son in the play:

So spineless, these fatherless brats—no dads, no discipline! Then he laughed, and Ellen couldn't take any more. Couldn't even say goodbye to anyone, just left.

Why were her feet so cold?

Because she went out in gym socks and holey patent-leather shoes in the middle of winter.

She was only nineteen years old and had written a whole play—that was pretty cool of her. And now it was going to be performed at the theater, and here she was—she, who otherwise dropped out of everything and had such social anxiety that she couldn't even get on a bus. She couldn't see the boundaries, didn't know where she began and other people ended.

When she got onto a bus full of strangers, she got sick to her stomach, broke out in a cold sweat. Someone would bump into her, accidentally, and she'd be terror stricken. The bus was full of meat and bones and blood and vibrated as one complete whole. Such horror. What part of it was hers and what was theirs? How was she supposed to know something that no one taught? What limbs belonged to her if she could feel all of them but at the same time, none of them?

Why were her feet so cold?

She stopped her car at the traffic light, opened the passenger-side door. That strange lady with the scar who was always looking at Ellen as though she were picking out something for dinner. Chomping her chewing gum with her mouth open and never breaking eye contact, coming and going as she pleased. She didn't want a ride with her. She'd rather walk all the way home in her gym socks, in the foamy ice water in her patent-leather shoes.

Ow, eee, she said when she took them off in the vestibule, and her mom came out of the long hallway from the kitchen. At the very end of the hall was a yellow Formica table, a yellow deck of cards, and yellow cigarettes that her mom put down in a yellow ashtray while she used her yellow fingers to leaf through yellow papers with yellow holes in them and yellow emotions that blended together with her yellow nails and the yellow cigarettes that were eternally burning between her fingers or in the ashtray and the yellow locks of hair that rested against her cheeks, spilled over her shoulders, her yellow dressing gown.

Oh, my sweet love, said her mom, helping Ellen out of her shoes.

Foot bath? she suggested, but Ellen said the sudden change would be too much.

But it'll only be bad for a moment, said her mom. Then you'll warm up and everything will be all better. It's good for rheumatism, too, and also for corns, if you have them.

I'm nineteen years old, Mama. Of course I don't have corns.

She answered because it was easier. Even though she knew her mom just said whatever and never heard anything she said. If Ellen stopped answering, her mom would just keep on saying whatever. An interminable whatever based on nothing whatsoever.

Age has nothing to do with it, said her mom. It might also be a good idea to moisten your feet and then wrap them in wool, prop them up on the radiator, and go to sleep. Corns are often like tangled yarn—you just have to find the right spot to pull . . .

Then she disappeared back into all that yellow, faded into the smoke and pages and cards.

Ellen looked out her bedroom window and over the bay. The Search and Rescue squad was running a training drill with neon buoys and emergency flares and blinking lights in the winter darkness. Two days out in the world and her feet had nearly frozen off. Three more days of this and she'd be frozen through. When the heat penetrated her numbness, it hurt.

The director had said that she had to sit in with them for the first week, and then she could decide how often she'd come in after that. Door was always open. Two of five days were over and done with. She wasn't going to spend one more minute there.

That night, she sat in the living room with her mom while they unpicked a sweater together. An old sweater of her father's that had started to fray and that her mom wanted to reuse the yarn from. Because all things come with a story, and sometimes, stories are changed by a thing.

Let's say, shall we, that this sweater continued to hang in the closet, her mom said, and let's say that there was a fire in the building and the sweater got burned up, then the story might change in your head, even though it'd already come to an end, said Mom, and Ellen listened, because it was easier. She'd tried not listening, and that was worse.

I once had a girlfriend who gave me a necklace. Where did you get this necklace? I asked her, but she didn't want to tell me, and so I never wore it until one night. It was green and matched my dress. Malachite, I remember. And that evening, I met my friend's ex-husband and fell in love with him. You remember Ársæll, don't you? I didn't understand it until long after. Long after my friend had stopped talking to me and Ársæll was gone. Malachite. I hung the necklace on the trash can, and it blended right in because the trash can was all dark green and flecked like malachite, too. See, he'd originally given her the necklace, and my friend wouldn't dream of wearing it after they divorced. It reminded her so much of him that she gave it to me.

What are you going to do with the yarn? Ellen asked her mom. She was wrapping a skein around her hands while her mom gently pulled out the stitches.

I'm going to attach it to his headstone somehow.

His headstone?

Yes, that's what I've been picturing.

They're just going to get rid of it . . . or it'll get blown away.

They were Álfur's widow and their three children. They got rid of everything that Ellen's mom put on his grave, and then she'd blow things out of proportion and get really agitated. Then Ellen would sit beside her and comfort her:

All things end in the sea, she said.

In the landfill, said her mom.

The landfill is in the sea, said Ellen.

Then we are in the sea, said her mom.

We are in the sea, said Ellen.

Everything is clean in the sea, said her mom.

Everything is always moving in the sea, said Ellen.

Ellen didn't know her half-siblings. Sometimes she saw them on arts programs on TV or heard them on the radio talking about their dad. Her dad. They were all literary scholars or cultural managers and working to preserve their father's legacy.

For example, they erected a memorial in his honor next to the lighthouse at Grótta and opened a museum in his home. Then they established a foundation that gave out an award for the best poem.

The best poem.

When Ellen was nine years old, she submitted a poem to the competition. Her mom read it over and said that she was definitely going to win.

> *The skies crack*
> *when god gets fat.*
> *The moon is a gash*
> *the clouds, trash.*

They looked at the envelope and saw your name and that's why you didn't get the award. I just know that's why! said her mother, crying. Ellen wasn't so sure. She read the poem again and didn't think it was clever anymore, just rather childish.

Every year for the next seven years—or until the year she turned sixteen—Ellen submitted poems that gradually became better. Her mom was always equally enthusiastic. But she especially loved the last one—

> *I swallowed the stone that you gave me*
> *big enough to choke on*
> *or just about*
> *so heavy that when I jumped*
> *I fell hard*
> *and sunk*
> *deep*
> *but light enough that*
> *I sprang back up*

gasping for breath
and bit
the hook you threw out
not necessarily to me
but you know
and when it sliced into my gums
it lodged itself tight
and I bled
but still not enough
and the stone was heavy enough
that the line snapped
and I wondered
as I dragged myself ashore
about the will to live
innate
because it seems to be
unquenchable
and about what you were doing
at that very moment
if you were bored
if you were setting out thumbtacks
gluing the door shut
shoving tinfoil in the keyholes
sketching out someone else's
internal struggle
with blood from your own veins
or blacking out the windows with
trash bags
or if maybe you were cultivating something
under infrared lights
something that closes in the daylight
and opens at night

something that awakens within all of this
bottled-up phobia fearful foolish
bloodless
and the soles of my feet press down into the sand
and then lift and walk ashore with me
and I remember that that's where we met
and I remember that that's where we saw each other
and I remember that that's where we said goodbye
and I remember that that's where we slept
and I remember that that's where we were infected
but I don't remember if we were cured
and I don't know where you went
and I break the bottle you gave me and the perfume
snap the necklace you gave me and the pearls
I rip out my teeth and my hands
are no longer the hands
that grope for you in the darkness
grasping at nothing and groping
after something in the nothingness
they found something in the nothingness
something inhuman and cold
in the nothingness

—which didn't win either, and her mom cried and said the reason Ellen hadn't won was that *she was who she was.* Ellen read the poem again and understood all too well why she hadn't won. She didn't think the poem was powerful anymore, just rather adolescent.

The poem was about a boy she met on the internet. They chatted at night after Ellen had gotten in bed, and sometimes she got messages from him during the day, short videos of noisy engines in his uncle's auto repair shop or a sneaker-wearing foot crushing an aluminum can until it disappeared.

After a few weeks of this, she wanted to meet him in person, but it was like he hadn't seen her message. She mentioned it a few more times before he agreed and suggested that they go for ice cream. She got there before him, took a seat and fiddled with her phone, and then finally saw him come in, almost exactly as she'd imagined him—a gangly, long-haired boy with long limbs, the arms of his jacket and legs of his pants a little too short.

He caught sight of her and smiled, reddened a little, and she smiled back. When he sat down and asked whether he could buy her an ice cream, she stretched her hand across the table. When her fingertips touched his cheek, he moved away. Ellen was sweating under a thick layer of pressed powder. Her mask itched, and the boy asked why she'd done that.

I just wanted to pat you on the cheek, she said, thinking that she sounded like some kind of perv—a pressed-powdered perv who had dry patches flaking off her face, a perv with flecks of dried spit at the corners of her mouth, a perv with crumbs in her makeup and fruit flies hovering around her head.

Ellen was sure he'd call the whole thing off, now that he'd seen her in person and realized what a perv she was, but then he grabbed her knee and squeezed it under the table. His hair dangled down his back between his shoulder blades, but he clearly never brushed it, so it was just one big tangle.

Why don't you brush your hair? Ellen giggled, and then his smile disappeared. He narrowed his eyes at her, hardened his grip on her knee.

They usually met during the day, when Ellen should have been in school, and drove around in his car drinking lukewarm beer, smoking cigarettes, making out, or else just sat and said nothing. He didn't have a steady job, instead lived at home with his parents and took on odd jobs in his uncle's garage.

Sometimes, she went to his house. His room was small and didn't actually have anything in it other than a bed, a desk, two computers and cords, and then this green plastic bucket that didn't make any sense at all. It was a bucket like one of those that kids play with in sandboxes and he'd laid a cake plate over the top of it, like a lid.

What do you have in the bucket? asked Ellen, and he said there was a frog in the bucket.

A frog! repeated Ellen in surprise, and she wanted to look in the bucket, but he got a serious expression on his face and shook his head. Then he turned off the light and played Simon & Garfunkel's "The Sound of Silence" at full blast. Ellen sat still in the darkness and waited for her eyes to adjust or for him to touch her, but neither happened.

She wanted to go home but knew she'd regret it as soon as she did. As soon as she left, she'd have him on the brain, him and all the strange things he said and did and which she'd then try to puzzle together and understand what he wanted or didn't want until finally, she'd be totally mixed up and wheezing like a nervous pug and unable to sit still. And then she'd have to do something. It wouldn't matter what. Just something. Send him a video of a cat wearing a lion costume. A squawking parrot.

The anticipation. She'd sit, transfixed in the silent, stark light of day and see people all around her. Other kids her age would be talking about standardized tests and summer jobs and something else she wouldn't catch. It wouldn't interest her. She'd just sit there until she couldn't help but do something else, like send him another message. Then maybe he'd answer.

He never suggested they hang out. He didn't kiss her the first time he had the chance. She must be a perv. Some kind of pushy creeper with unusual needs.

She sat in the darkness and waited. She could just make out the shape of him and saw that he was lying on the floor with his head under his desk. As soon as "The Sound of Silence" ended, she asked if maybe they should do it.

He lay totally motionless and said nothing. For a moment, she wondered if he'd heard her, and then the next thing that occurred to her was that maybe he was pretending to be asleep. So he could spare her the answer or else spare himself having to answer.

Have you . . . before? he asked finally.

No, she whispered.

Okay, he said, but is it okay if we do it later? I'm so tired.

Okay, she said, and forced herself to leave.

She let three days go by without sending him a message, which was a record. When she finally called to ask if she could come over, it felt like months had passed, and she couldn't understand how he could sound so indifferent.

Sure, whatever, he said after a short silence. Sure she could come over, but he had to finish something first.

Maybe I'll just call you later, okay? he said, suddenly in a hurry and not waiting for a reply.

Okay, said Ellen, to the dial tone.

That night, she took the bus to his house. She didn't call ahead—she'd made up her mind to see him. His mom let her in, and she took off her shoes and coat in the vestibule, slipped through the suffocating scent of fried lamb fat, Sunday supper, and went upstairs, her heart pounding wildly as she knocked on his bedroom door.

The cold expression on his face didn't shift when he saw her, but he pawed at her head, stroking her hair and cupping his hands over her ears, tucking her head down into his arms, and Ellen felt his warmth, smelled the scent of sleep, of boy, of T-shirts, of sweet sweat, and she didn't want him to let go, wanted to go on resting there just like that, imagining that his body was her body, too, and thereby escaping herself and forgetting and being forgotten.

Then he gently pushed her away and said he needed to finish something, but that it was fine if she wanted to hang out there while he did.

The ceiling light was on in the bedroom. Beyond the door, she could hear the clattering of the dishes as his mom washed up, the nightly news jingle on TV. His back was turned to her and he hammered on his keyboard. She sat on his bed. His hair was so tightly woven in such a dense tangle that it reminded her of a beaver's tail she'd seen in some nature documentary, damming a river at night.

She lost her patience, got to her feet and walked over to him, gently clasping the tangle and saying she could get the knots out if he wanted. He jumped, pulled away from her touch.

You never want to see me, said Ellen.

I was helping my friend . . .

Would you rather help him than *do it* with me?

He didn't answer, but loosened her grip, started to turn back around to his computer.

Why exactly are you with me? Ellen asked.

She happened to look at the screen, black with unreadable sentences that quickly scrolled by. On the desk there was a pile of computer cords and another computer with a black screen and some neon green thing blinking on it. Then she saw the bucket with the cake plate on top of it.

Before she had a chance to think, she snatched the plate and looked into the bucket. There was a shriveled frog at the bottom of it, no bigger than a matchbox.

Its legs stretched out from its gaunt corpse, and Ellen smelled the faint stench of rot.

He immediately grabbed the plate from her hands, put it back on top of the bucket, and slapped her face.

Not to hurt her.

As if to chastise a small child.

The boxes stood in the middle of the living room floor. I turned on the nightly news and walked around them a few times, but then all of a sudden stopped short because I remembered the exact moment that my grandma died. She'd been a bud on a branch that would have otherwise ended bare and spindly. *Bling*, said a leaf, then propagated and died. At that very second, I tugged at the moment in which my mother was born and then died, the moment in which I was born and will die. The moment I die has not yet come to pass, and yet, I tugged at it, somewhere in the future.

I lit a cigarette and immediately remembered the sweater. Rough wool yarn that pulled taut around Mama's fingers as she knitted. She started knitting when she stopped smoking and the sweater was for me.

Would the sweater be in the box? I wondered. Then Mama's blood would be in the box. My mother's DNA in the box. Her one-of-a-kind composition in the box.

The boxes were from a grocery store. *Ora canned green beans. Johnson's baby powder. Packets of just-add-water soup mix.* They had been labeled before, but the labels had been crossed out. Then they'd been labeled again.

On the TV, there was an image of a butchered whale carcass. I looked out the window and saw that there was a man on the steps I didn't recognize. A white, unmarked delivery van in the driveway. I went to the door.

Good evening, I said, regarding the man—expressionless and middle-aged, pale, wearing a parka and gloves.

I've come to pick up the boxes, he said in a flat voice.

The boxes?

The boxes you found in your grandma's basement, he said.

But they have my name on them, I said. They're my boxes.

The man didn't answer; his expression didn't change.

Well, okay then, I said and opened the door wide. The man didn't take off his shoes when he came in. He walked straight into the living room, picked up the first box, and carried it out to the van.

What's in them? I asked when he came back in to pick up the next box, but he just gazed at me like a cabbage and didn't answer. He took the last two at the same time, stacked them in the back of the van, and next thing I knew, he was driving away without looking at me or saying goodbye.

I went back into the living room; it was time to get to work. I had a fiberglass mold of a girl in her teens in the basement. It teetered down there, propped up on one edge, and I went and got it, lugged it back up the steep stairs. I cleared off the dining room table and put the mold down on top of it, opening it so that the negative space of the girl appeared before me.

I have absolutely no memory of her name, the director's daughter who volunteered to be cast in plaster. It took an entire day. Then I made a fiberglass mold to keep. The script revolved around a pedophile who ordered himself a silicone doll on the internet that looked like a child. Endless ethical questions, crushingly dull. But the doll came out really well, if I do say so myself.

How old must the girl be now? Maybe twenty, but there's her body, unchanged.

I could see *feigð*, someone's death approaching, and generally knew when I'd said goodbye to a person for the last time. Actually, I was wrong sometimes. But right more often than wrong.

Feigð wasn't visible in a physical sense, although if asked, I'd try to back myself up with a color or light or something that flickered. I didn't see anything, but thought:

Soon, you will die.

The thought was part of me. There wasn't some voice that whispered this to me. No colors. No flickers. I simply thought:

Soon, you will die.

And more often than not, I was right. In retrospect, I'd think that maybe the person in question had a color on their skin that might have given me a clue. I racked my brain for a logical explanation—an illness I'd heard people around me talking about and subconsciously absorbed. But yellow colors wouldn't explain accidental deaths any better.

When I saw Ellen's father for the last time, I knew it:

Soon, I thought, you will die.

We'd met when I was working on the set of one of his plays, and we also went around with the same people. We didn't really have any reason to talk to one another, but we'd say hi and sometimes, like that last time, we'd stop and chitchat for a moment.

It was around noon on a Sunday in the winter of 2000, the day bitter cold and still. A smattering of snow that crunched underfoot, and I was lighting a cigarette when I saw him turn onto the street, looking tired. When he was right in front of me, he recognized me and said hello, then hesitated and finally came to a stop.

I registered a smell—hot, aggressive, accumulated. An old smell of long, sordid nights, a *brennivín*-laced tobacco smell. A smell of iron. A sweet smell of chaos, bedrooms and smoke and crotches and smacks—muffled, sweaty, repetitive.

You got a cigarette? he asked hoarsely, and I gave him one, lit it for him. He shuddered with the first drag. He was probably cold in his shirt and thin wool jacket. Plaid. Then I thought:

Soon, you will die.

You're always up at the theater, aren't you? he asked, and I said yes, for the most part—I was always making props. I didn't ask anything in return, was very aware of that lack of anything to say that had characterized all our interactions. We fell silent. He had a distant look on his face when he said goodbye.

I will never see you again, I thought, and one week later I listened to the news of his passing on the radio. I sat at the kitchen table at home, rolling cigarettes with a special device I'd purchased in Copenhagen. I filled the silver case of mine that had room for ten, which made it easier for me to keep track of how much I was smoking than just rolling them one at a time. I wanted to quit.

> *The writer Álfur Finnsson has died at only fifty-nine years of age. Álfur was one of the most esteemed writers of his generation and leaves behind a prodigious body of work from his prolific career. Eleven novels, ten plays, and five books of poetry, as well as short stories and essay*

collections. His work has been translated into many languages, and he's won the Icelandic Literary Prize multiple times, as well as the Nordic Council Literature Prize . . .

Álfur leaves behind his wife and three children.

Four, I thought, shook my head and shuddered, recalling the blue of his face.

I didn't know Álfur's widow, Laufey, very well. We had all gone to the same high school. Laufey had studied nursing, but since then had mostly dedicated herself to domestic duties, which later evolved into her taking care of assorted business for her husband. She was his agent, secretary, and self-appointed protector. After he died, her work was nowhere near done and, if anything, her activities increased.

They weren't together during his final years. I didn't know the details, of course. Had heard different things but didn't know what was true and what were lies. There'd always been stories about him going around. She was definitely in art school—the girl he met. Thirty-five years younger than him, and together they had Ellen. His fourth child, who Laufey neglected to mention in his obituary. Ellen, the same name as the main character in Álfur's first novel. The one who died of a broken heart or tuberculosis or something like that.

I'd never been much of a fan of Álfur Finnsson's work, by the way. I thought he was overrated and his fan base a function of wishful thinking more than anything else, but that was definitely just me. I was never much for dramas, any more than for rom-coms or action films.

I divided the body into segments, according to where it was supposed to have been sawed into pieces with a rusty, old saw. At the neck, arms, legs, and knees. I got some clay, flung it on the table a few times, and then softened it in my hands.

After that, I sat and sculpted without thinking, trusting my body to know its own features implicitly. The fingers know better than the mind how a wound on a sawed-apart neck feels to the touch, knows the thickness of skin, how fat bursts, where bones are and how they break.

When the seven clay segments were ready, I blended the plaster. I poured it into a shallow basin and spread Vaseline on the clay before I put the plaster over it. The next day, I'd cut them out and mix up more plaster. Submerge the other side of the clay in the plaster before going to the theater for the table reading.

Everyone had arrived but her. The director, Hreiðar, looked unrested and irritated, the hair on the back of his head unkempt, and he was on edge about every little thing. I had worked with him on numerous occasions, recognized these ups and downs of his, and knew what to avoid. The set designer, on the other hand, seemed all too oblivious to the situation and peppered him with questions about this or that detail until Hreiðar finally lost it and yelled at her. Then there was silence.

He was really preoccupied with power. He always sized someone up when he met them for the first time. If he deemed the person in question to be on a lower rung of the prestige ladder than he was, he gave himself leave to bark and snarl. If, on the other hand, he presumed the person possessed something he needed, he was fawning and slavering.

He'd kiss the ring entirely unbidden whenever he got the chance, but still wanted to be called a courageous and radical artist. Sometimes it's hard for those who have it all to have to pick and choose.

The actors made the best of the silence, wanted to start discussing the play even though Ellen hadn't shown, but then she tumbled through the door wearing the exact same clothes as the day before even though it had, if anything, gotten colder.

Hreiðar applauded and welcomed her. Ellen took a seat on the arm of a chair, said she was sick and that she might have to leave early today, too. Her nose was red, and she was wearing a pair of glasses that were taped together in the middle with a Band-Aid.

You wear glasses? asked the set designer, and a look of horror crossed Ellen's face.

No, she said. I don't, actually. Then she stuck the glasses in her backpack, took out a printed copy of the play and a gnawed-on pen.

Jæja, said the director. We'll start where we left off last time, on page fourteen.

Everyone flipped to the page. Ellen, too.

> SON:
> *When you came home at night, all of us crawled behind*
> *the television set and laughed into cans and urinated on*
> *the VCR—a wriggling heap back there, all your many*
> *children . . .*

Etc.

As the actors read the play and I heard it for the first time, I realized the script was not remotely as good as people wanted to believe it was. There were some really fine segments, and the overall structure wasn't terrible, but even so, there were a number of elements that could have stood to be improved, on top of which, I thought two of the characters were unnecessary. Superfluous. She would have done better to focus on the relationship between the father and son, instead of trotting out the uncle and the grandfather, who played no special role in the plot.

Ellen had tucked her hair behind her bright red ears. That's where she blushed, I saw, rather than in her cheeks. It was as if she was constantly sinking deeper into herself as the actors read. She had closed her eyes and was pressing her thin lips together. When the director motioned for the actors to stop the reading so he could make some notes, she didn't even notice.

Would we say that this is the first turning point? he asked thoughtfully, and the set designer suggested that it came earlier, right at the top of page seventeen.

It would be nice to hear what Ellen has to say about this, said Hreiðar, staring at her.

Ellen?

Huh?

Whether the first turning point happens there, on page twenty. When the son enters with the boa constrictor?

Turning point? asked Ellen obtusely.

Yes . . . whether that's the first . . . dramatic beat—pivot.

I have no idea what you're talking about, said Ellen. I didn't sleep at all last night.

Weakness. I watched the director's face carefully. Would he think Ellen didn't give a shit about him, or would he realize that she was insecure and didn't know how to talk about a script's dramatic beats?

Of course she didn't. She was just a teenager.

Contempt stirred in the director's mind, snuffed out the glint in his eyes, which turned a dull matte.

You wrote the play. Did you not? he said with affected friendliness.

I don't know, Ellen choked out. Maybe not, maybe I didn't write any of it.

Then she stormed out. Clumsily, knocking into her chair and shutting the door behind her with unnecessary force.

Erg . . . groaned the oldest actor, conflict averseness radiating from his face.

The director collected himself.

Let's continue the reading, he said, smiling blandly and putting on his glasses, clearing his throat.

I looked out the window, saw how the snowflakes were showering down from the dirt-gray clouds, melting as soon as they touched the dirt-gray slush that blanketed the ground. A shivery, sleet-filled hourglass.

Aren't you going to call her? I asked all of a sudden, much to my own surprise.

Are you talking to me? asked Hreiðar.

You were rude. Aren't you going to apologize?

I saw the anger well up in him, but he acted as though he hadn't heard me, and the actors kept reading:

FATHER:
Beautiful floor. Is it a new floor? Am I . . . Am I mixing things up?

SON:
No—it's a totally new floor.

FATHER:
Is it that distressed pine?

SON:
. . . Noooo, it's actually laminate. Very high quality, some kind of hard parquet . . .

FATHER:
Formaldehyde. Parquet is made out of the poison form-aldehyde. Swedish contrivance.

SON:
Poison, yes . . .

FATHER:
Yes, and there's also some strange odor in here—is it damp?

SON:
Yes, it's maybe a little damp.

FATHER:
Mold?

SON:
Noooooo. I think not.

FATHER:
I've gotten very ill living in moldy houses.

SON:
Nuh-uh.

FATHER:
Oh, yeah-huh. Some illnesses sneak up on you, slow and corrosive. What's that noise?

SON:
What noise?

FATHER:
That noise.

SON:
I honestly don't hear a thing.

FATHER:
Like mold squelching between the planks.

SON:
C'mon, Dad.

FATHER:
Where are you going, by the way—why are you wearing that suit? And with your goatee in a ponytail? I can't understand why you went bald so young. No one in my family went bald. Your great-grandfather? He died with a mane, like a lion—almost a hundred years old.

SON:
I've got a date.

GRANDFATHER:
He's hoping she'll be there.

FATHER:
Who is she?

GRANDFATHER:
Eh, she's one of those depressive types. Works in reception, I think.

FATHER:
Does he have a chance?

GRANDFATHER:
It's the annual work to-do. Everyone's got a chance.

SON:
She's a lawyer. She works in accounting.

FATHER:
The annual work party, eh? Can I come?

SON:
I don't think anyone's bringing their parents.

FATHER:
Not even the singles?

SON:
No, spouses aren't even coming.

FATHER:
I'm sure it'll be fine if your Uncle Konni and I pop by.

SON:
You and Konni?

FATHER:
Yeah, Konni's on his way over.

SON:
But I'm just about to leave.

FATHER:

*Hurry up and find those wrenches and then I'll be on
my way.*

SON:
Dad, you never lent me any wrench set . . .

FATHER:
Am I just going crazy?

SON:
*He'll never leave, will he? And if he does leave, he'll just
come right back again?*

GRANDFATHER:
You may have to kill him.

SON:
Kill him?

GRANDFATHER:
*Yes, or at least, that would be the most typical thing to
do in your position.*

SON:
Yes, but wouldn't it be a little too typical?

GRANDFATHER:
*What if everyone went around thinking like that? Then
there'd be no patricide and you know exactly what that
would mean.*

SON:
What would that mean?

GRANDFATHER:
Just use that wrench set.

SON:
He never lent me any wrench set—there's no wrench set here. He just always pretends to be picking up a wrench set, but there is no wrench set. I don't even know what that is. Wrench set?

GRANDFATHER:
You have to use your imagination.

Sometimes, it was like I could turn myself off, screw myself all the way down and then simply extinguish. A lifeless stain in my place. No one cared. I sidled out and doubt that the director took any notice. I figured the next time he glanced over he'd be surprised to see no one in my seat.

It didn't cross my mind to offer her a ride, but I did want to follow her. The feeling was similar to my feigð suspicions. I wanted to interfere, prevent the inevitable.

I don't generally give in to this longing. You can't warn people of their own deaths. And anyway, what if I was wrong?

I didn't see feigð on Ellen, but I wanted to follow her, and that longing I gave in to. She walked all the way back home, to an apartment building near the sea, let herself in, and locked the door behind her. She probably lived there with her mom, whose name I couldn't remember for the life of me.

I keyed her address into the online directory and turned up a number of names, but not Ellen's—just her mom's. I remembered the woman's name as soon as I saw it. Lilja Guðlaugsdóttir. A name that somehow split in two on your lips, filled with air.

The one time I saw her, I was struck by how childlike she was. Her facial features were such that she could have played a child in the theater long past thirty, and her voice, too, which was high and pinched, like in a cartoon. It automatically made you want to look down to check if she had her shoes on the right feet.

The sight of her threading her arm through that of a man as brutish as Álfur Finnsson must have been downright indecent. That's why people talked about it so much. Emotional speculation was what made the news, questions that were never answered.

And why was he inclined to take up with a child?

Was there something in his books that hinted at this?

Such *inclinations*.

But she wasn't a child. She was a woman of at least twenty-four years of age, in art school, and, as I remember someone saying at the time, it was unkind to judge her on her appearance. Maybe she was brilliant, loaded with experience—who could say?

Álfur refused to be ashamed, waltzed around town with her in tow, heavily pregnant, much to the distress of his wife. Lilja's hair reached down to her ass. Her steps feather light and pitter-pattery, an expression of perpetual astonishment on her childlike face. Her cheeks rosy.

All of a sudden, I heard a thump on the hood of the car. It was Ellen. She'd come out while I was using the internet to spy on her.

I rolled down the car window. She looked at me expectantly.

You planning on being here long? she finally asked, and I flinched.

I'm sorry, I said. I was worried about you and just followed, I know it seems crazy, but I meant well . . .

She regarded me dubiously. Looking much more like her father than her mother.

Why are you worried?

Because of how you stormed out . . . I don't know.

Okay, she said begrudgingly and hesitated. Okay. But get out of here now. And quit spying on me. It's the absolute last thing I need, some old lesbo obsessing over me.

I started the car and skidded out of the parking lot, drove straight home in the half-light, shamefaced, exhausted, and wanting to erase the last thing she said.

That was completely unnecessary.

Something was glinting in the twilight of the living room. I turned on the lights and saw that in the middle of the floor, where the boxes had been, something tiny and glass was glinting. I crept over cautiously, feeling my heart hammering in my chest.

Was that what I thought it was?

No.

It couldn't be.

I went cold in an instant. When I reached out, my palms were sweaty, my fingers quivered so much that I could hardly manage to catch hold of the horse. The glass horse. I couldn't catch my breath, clutching it in my sweaty palm and swerving across the living room floor. Still wearing my coat.

I had to get out. The horse had to go. I spun on my heels and lurched back out to the car with the horse jingling in my pocket.

Without thinking, I drove west toward the sea and wondered if there was a way for me to effectively destroy the horse. Nothing seemed entirely satisfactory. Chucking it into the toilet could mean it getting lodged somewhere in the pipes, which was a chilling prospect. Flinging it into the sea could mean it getting tangled in seaweed and from then on out, always being there, just offshore.

Fastening it to a rock slab and grinding it down with a stone until there was nothing left but some crumbs of glass. Grinding the crumbs until they became a fine powder, blowing it into the sea. Would the sea then become a horse?

I also didn't understand how the horse could have fallen out of one of the boxes and lain there on the floor for all that time. Without my noticing it. It seemed too loathsome to be a coincidence. The light from the traffic splayed across my face in the twilight, and for a moment I was gripped by terror.

Did I dare, generally speaking, break the horse? I knew very well that there was nothing to fear. Of course nothing would happen if the glass broke. And yet I suspected that the physical material itself had certain archival properties. Of course I knew that glass was just glass. A thing just a thing. But I worked with things. Body parts of resin, horns of rubber, and masks that could speak. Material that flowed out of my hands, took on a fixed form, fell apart once again.

Of course I knew that glass wasn't a living thing. Of course glass *was* a living thing. The sea could become glass. A horse tail the size of a sperm whale rising out of the depths, undulating amid a splintering chorus, and disappearing below the surface once again. Maybe it would be best to preserve the horse in its unaltered state, to hide it, forget it.

Could it then reappear somewhere else later? Suddenly? A glittering mass? I parked the car out by the Grótta lighthouse and lit a cigarette, my fourth cigarette of the day, and felt the horse in my pocket without touching it—it radiated heat.

Would I always associate this place with the horse? Would I never again be able to come out to Grótta? When I was done with the cigarette, I drove off again. I got the idea to grind the horse into a powder and put it in an envelope, send it somewhere.

Send it to him.

I nearly fainted at the idea. Of course I would never do anything like that. If I went to Hvalfjörður, would I then see the horse every time I stopped by Hvalfjörður? Its faint outline appearing in the back of my mind? If I went to Rauðavatn, would it always be like I was looking through frosted glass whenever Rauðavatn was mentioned?

Stuffing it down into a crevice in the highlands. Putting it in with the glass recyclables. Throwing it carelessly into the trash. The whole world would be a suspect.

It was in moments like these that I missed having a friend. Someone I could call up and confer with. As soon as the idea rang out in my head, I felt a despair that was accompanied by a pip from my phone. I figured it was work related, but it was Ellen.

I didn't meat to be a cunt.

I stared at the message.

Didn't meat to be a cunt.

The phone beeped again.

mean.

One morning, when I'd planned to stop by the house and putter about with something or other on my to-do list, I realized that everything was finished. I had practically rebuilt the whole house all by myself, and I still remember that feeling. The pride. It was my house. My fingerprints were everywhere—inside the pipes, the drain, on the back of the wood panels.

When I lived in Copenhagen, I often went to Filmhuset to see avant-garde films. One of my favorite directors was John Waters, and I remember a scene from one of his first pictures, which he made with almost no funding whatsoever. In it, two people break into a middle-class home and lick everything. They lick the chairs, the table, the floor, the stairs, the banister; they lick the crockery, the pillows, the bric-a-brac—everything.

And I understood that feeling. Understood how important it is to be one with physical material, with the stuff things are made of, to become part of it. To be stuff. A coating of saliva. Greasy fingerprints. Shit in the pipes. Understood how someone else's fingerprints constrict your existence. There's nothing particularly charitable or charming about it, but it's human.

I took over that parcel of land. It was mine and I got bigger; on it, I filled up with all those particles that swirl and settle and encroach and embed themselves permanently in things. Become matter that can move, and thereby live.

And I was constantly getting more projects. My name became one of those that people automatically said when they needed someone who could construct a severed hand that could twitch.

It didn't take me long to pay down my loans and open a savings account, which I enjoyed watching grow. I wanted to travel around Asia. In Copenhagen, I'd met a woman from Burma. She'd emigrated from there with her parents around 1960.

She was a little older than me and was studying filmmaking. I was quite taken with her and helped her with little things when she was doing her final project—a feature-length film in which the main characters were plants, some wild, some not.

We were never really friends, but one evening at the end of shooting, we went with some others to Bo-bi Bar, had beer and boiled eggs and sat chain-smoking and drinking and chatting, and she, though usually pretty withdrawn, told us about the situation in Burma.

During the fall of 1987, I took off six months from work and dipped into my savings account. I flew to Bangkok and from there to Burma, which was still called Burma then, although two years later they changed its name to Myanmar.

On my first day in Bangkok, I applied for a visa, sat in the back of a wagon attached to the back of a motorcycle called a tuk-tuk, which then darted between cars. I don't remember anything particularly well. Just that I was unrested and awestruck.

At the office, I filled out forms and discovered that I would not be allowed to stay in Burma for longer than a week, which was a disappointment. What I knew about the country was limited—just whatever I'd heard or read in magazines and books—and I realized that beneath that, a more complicated truth was hiding, a truth I never did come to understand.

I knew that the country had been under the control of a military dictatorship since 1962. That since then, the country had been cut off from the outside world.

I knew that the country was locked, and that the people were locked in.

In my mind, Burma was lavish opulence: dark green mountains, rice paddies in the mist, the outlines of water buffalo, egg-shaped golden temples that looked like they'd been pulled up out of the earth by a giant hand. Massive religious statuary toppled in the jungles. Red-clad monks walking out of the sunset, single file.

If it weren't for the stuff I was made of, I would have never stopped traveling. The world would have become a mold and I would have poured into it, would have become a grain of sand in a shell, a pearl in a beach vendor's strand, around the neck of a woman, tapping lightly on her skin and stretching taut over her collarbone when she moved.

On my first day, I met Khin the tour guide outside my guesthouse in Yangon. We traveled by bus or I sat on the back of his motor scooter, and he showed me convents deep in the jungle, introduced me to a monk who walked with a golden staff, an herbalist, and a snake that, according to folk belief, was the daughter of a monk who had died a hundred years earlier.

The snake lay motionless on an altar in a special chamber, atop a mountain of coins and paper bills, enormous and ancient. It was looked after by a young mute girl, her cheeks and forehead painted white. Tears running from her eyes, she showed me pictures and statuettes of the daughter of the holy man who reposed there, in snake form.

Khin told me this girl had run her mouth, spoken about something she'd seen, and that's why she'd lost her tongue and why she cried like she did.

When he spoke, he tended to lower his voice, bend down to me—as if he were fixing his shoes, even—and whisper.

We were followed by a man. He shadowed our every step and matched each of the tour guide's movements. Sometimes, he sat a short distance away from us and once, when he seemed to be lost in his own thoughts, Khin took his opportunity.

In an instant, he asked me to listen carefully. His dark eyes flashed close to my own, and he spoke quickly:

They come into small, remote villages, he said, fill vans with people . . .

Quick as he could, he lifted his shirt and showed me scars. Proof, he whispered with a grimace. The white scars disrupted the pattern of the bamboo tattoos that encased his chest and stomach.

The man who followed us was no apparition. He was slender and delicately built, like Khin, wearing a pressed, white, short-sleeve button-down and a long, clay-brown skirt that was wrapped around his loins, chewing on betel nuts and occasionally spitting out a blood-red cud.

The star of the movie was suddenly in my living room. I was so absorbed in the clay that I'd forgotten I was expecting him. So I must have left the front door open, and when he said hello, I nearly leapt out of my skin.

He apologized and then shook my hand and introduced himself. Betúel Benóný. I'd never met him in person. He was bigger than I'd expected, definitely over six feet, and his head was unusually broad, which was peculiar, given how doll faced he was. Something about his proportions made him seem smaller in photos, smaller and more delicate. I took hold of his hand in the air and scrutinized it—the hair that grew on his wrists and the backs of his hands reached all the way to his fingers.

Are you going to be this hairy in the movie? I asked without introducing myself in return, and he laughed, said as far as he knew.

It's important, I insisted and said that he couldn't let them shave him at the last minute.

I got a few rolls of plaster gauze and a tub with lukewarm water, then pointed for him to sit down and take the shoe and sock off of his left foot. Once I'd slathered his right hand with Vaseline, I first moistened the gauze and then slapped it around his wrist. His hand was encased before long and then I got a dollop of Vaseline and took hold of his big toe. It was hairy, too.

Eeee, now you're tickling me, he said with a smile, and I thought about what it must be like to be him. The most handsome, most talented, most sought-after, most adored, essential. His eyes met my own for a second, but he immediately looked away. No doubt worried I'd fall in love with him. No doubt always having to be careful. Always having to be careful with other people's hearts. Imagine being in possession of that kind of striking beauty, that kind of debilitating sex appeal.

Is this the first time you're playing the bad guy? I asked offhand and then remembered that he played a bad guy in a movie that had been a big hit of late. A serial killer, if I remembered correctly. But he wasn't pretentious in the least and told me all about the hit film as if it were normal that I'd never heard of it.

Then he talked about this Nordic crime picture and how he was particularly dreading a scene in which his character went sea swimming in the dead of winter. He said he was a real wimp when it came to the cold and that he'd already started preparing himself for the role, but it was going abysmally—he couldn't go any farther than up to his knees, even with the weather as mild as it had been of late.

You're just a regular charmer, aren't you? I blurted out. I hadn't actually meant to say that. The sentence echoed tartly in the air while I moved a hair dryer over the plaster.

Once he was gone, I would cut off his thumb and splice his big toe on in its place. Then I'd cast his hand in plaster and mix the silicone, make another mold. It's painstaking work and I'd lose myself entirely in it. Silicone is odorless, but even so, you can't paint in the same room in which you're creating a silicone cast because then the paint won't dry in the meantime. When it comes to this stuff, the smell doesn't tell the whole story.

I'd end up having to use a little dish soap to get the hand out of the mold, applied in five thin layers, and it would be really late by the time I went to sleep. My head would have gotten heavy, and my forehead would be throbbing. I'd regret not having gone down into the basement. I did that more and more seldom these days and didn't even open the windows. A kind of apathy rather than an impulse to self-destruct.

Was not caring an impulse?

When the silicone mold was ready, I'd pour dish soap into it and then shake the hand so it would spread all over. Then I'd prick tiny holes in the fingertips so that no air bubbles would form. I would make a support shell out of plaster and then pour the silicone into the mold, into the hand.

When the hand had dried and I could take off its mold like a glove, I would blend the dye with the thin liquid silicone that I'd use to paint the hand. I'd saw across the eye of an incredibly thin sewing needle, creating a fork, and stick the point of the needle into a tiny shard of wood that I'd use as a handle, jabbing dark hairs up to their hilts in Betúel Benóný's hand.

I'd thread narrow tubes into the shaft, make it so they reached all the way to the fingertips, and pump them full of blood-red liquid that would pool in the fingertips. We'd use these tubes on set—they'd be connected to other, longer ones, and I'd be positioned offscreen, and when I got the signal, I'd pump them so that blood would splutter out of the wrist when the hand was chopped off.

All in accordance with the script.

The lead actor would get a sulky look on his face when he saw me, relating, within my hearing, how I'd mocked him and his self-aggrandizements. That's how I took it when people shared *charming* stories about themselves with me. A lot of fucking ego masturbation, and I didn't want to know about it. The very thought enraged me.

He wanted to drag me into his everyday and tell me all his tedious news.

Undealable.

Unconsiderant.

Untolerable.

He acted like he hadn't heard what I said. The next time our eyes met, there was a visible warmth in his expression—a mischievousness, even—and I wasn't sure anymore what I'd said out loud and what I'd only thought.

At the end of the week, I flew back to Thailand from Burma. Checked myself into an inexpensive guesthouse in Bangkok and unpacked my luggage. The room was full of mosquitoes, and I turned on the fan, sealed the door with a wet towel, and went berserk with another, swatting and swatting until everything was covered with splotches of blood.

Night had fallen. The sidewalks were teeming with people selling food and trinkets. I couldn't move an inch without touching something or someone. If I wanted to cross a street, the only way I could ensure that drivers would stop was to make eye contact with them.

The layout of the city astonished me. The streets were long and wide, and it was rare to find an egress without hopping on the back of a motor scooter or onto a bus. The food stalls were on the sidewalks or in parking lots or halfway into the street. Sometimes, they'd set out plastic chairs under an awning. In my memory, the plastic chairs are child sized and my knees bent at an unnatural angle, the ground close; the stench of sewage comes back to me.

Everything blurred together in the heat. The contact with all those unknown people. *Germs* is the word that comes to mind. Bacteria and viruses and germs that flow between open glands and converge and blend with sweat and blood and tears and pus and shit. I felt nauseous and often hankered for a cold breeze. To shut down. Die.

I passed many days without speaking to a single person. I woke, ate breakfast at the hotel—a handful of rice and sautéed vegetables. Other than me, there were precious few guests and they only stopped there briefly. Usually men with a distant gleam in their eyes, on their way to Pattaya.

Some men pretended not to see me, but others wanted to chat. When I think about it now, I imagine that in their minds I became some kind of proxy for all Western women. They wanted me to understand them and sometimes outlined their cases to me as if they were standing before a judge. As a rule, they talked about exes. About their stinginess, their greed, their coldness, their pushiness, and they told me about their loneliness and their fear of the pointlessness of everything, of death.

They just wanted to feel alive and Thai women weren't like Western ones, they all said. These Thais didn't want anything in return, except, of course, some small remuneration, nothing much by the men's standards, but after that, they didn't constantly demand things the men didn't have to offer. Fidelity and intimacy and security and promises about one thing or another.

These Thais, said one man, understand that sex is sex. Sex is enough in and of itself. A freestanding event. And then another. With someone else. As long as they got paid. And they were tender, submissive. Not like The Ex. The sex drive is just a primal instinct, like eating and sleeping. It's a normal part of life and why shouldn't I allow myself to satisfy a natural urge? Sex is such a perfectly natural part of life—I delivered the mail, delivered the mail to a million houses, a million times my eyes scanned the address on a letter that by the grace of the muscles in my arms was delivered, and I always slept alone and hard and cold and

I cried in my sleep because I wasn't allowed to cry when I was awake. Another natural urge I wasn't allowed to satisfy. And I filled with fluids and I arrived here in Asia a hard cyst swollen with accumulated semen and tears, neither of which was permitted to flow from my perfectly natural human glands. As if I were a monster for having sexual desires and a little bitch for crying and I just wanted, just longed to be a man who comes and cries, but I'd turned into a cyst, an old cyst that had to go to Thailand to be drained . . .

. . . he told me, and I listened and thought about primal instincts and natural urges.

Drinking.

Eating.

Sleeping.

Dying.

After that conversation, many ear-splitting days passed without me opening my mouth for anything other than shoving sticky grains of rice into it. I don't know why I was in Bangkok for so long, why I never got around to going up a mountain or to the beach. I didn't even do any sightseeing—no golden temples or cloisters, full of monks and peacocks.

Maybe I was so worn-out from my trip around Burma that guesthouse walls with taped-together wall sockets and dead mosquitoes were enough. In the evenings, I sometimes went to the clubs, ordered a Red Bull or a Krating Daeng, which is what they call it in Thailand, and sat at the bar. They crowded together, the men, and young nymphs sat on their laps and got them in the mood while they guzzled and laughed and shouted and forgot their loneliness and tamped down their fear of death.

What did they see when they looked at me? Nothing at all, I imagine. I served no purpose. Satisfied no natural urge. And what did their *girlfriends* see? Neither a woman nor a man, neither an answer nor a deficiency. At a club, at night, not wanting sex, or money, or alcohol.

Not needing dancing, or songs, or music. Maybe they saw me and wondered about my purposelessness.

But maybe that's exactly what I needed. Maybe this lack was precisely the reason I lingered in Bangkok. Sex, money, alcohol, dancing and songs and laughter. First and foremost, laughter. Why else was I staying in that neighborhood, why else did I seek out that neighborhood's clubs? Of course I needed songs and dancing. Laughter. Then I met Mike.

He was one of those men who stumbled upon the guesthouse, but he stayed a little longer than the rest. He would have been around sixty. At first, I couldn't perceive any difference between him and the others. The same khaki shorts, the same polo shirt, the same socks in the same sandals, the same turnip-white legs, shot through with blue.

He sat next to me one morning, and we started chatting. He said he'd bought a little house in Ko Samui without having ever laid eyes on it. This was the first time he'd been to Thailand, but he'd decided he was never going to leave.

Why Thailand? I asked, and he shrugged, said he couldn't come up with anything more original.

The food's good, he said. Then he asked if I'd seen the Wat Phra Kaew temple and suggested we go check it out together the next day. I was taken aback. I shook my head, but something within me awoke from its stupor, something I'd quieted that's supposed to kick and wriggle, and I accepted the invitation.

The market stalls on the path leading up to the temple specialized in prayer beads and plastic lockets with pictures of Buddhist monks. Heaps and mountains of holy trinkets. The vendors' expressions serious—pompous, I thought—sneering as Mike bought some prayer beads.

Are you religious? I asked, and he said he planned to become so in his new life.

Just like that, I said, and he said he'd always had the desire to believe, but he hadn't let himself do it.

Of all the things a person should deny himself, I said, and he fell silent. Maybe I offended him. Maybe I offended him a few times, but I always do that when I like a person a lot. Want to show them how clever I am, but then say something tactless.

We visited the Emerald Buddha, and then it started raining buckets. We ran through the downpour until we tumbled into a restaurant. I laughed. Nothing was funny, but I laughed and got this feeling of unreality. Saw us from afar. Our wet khaki clothing, our sandals, our hair. Like every other middle-aged couple visiting the Emerald Buddha and then it starts to rain, oh, shucks.

That's probably what sparked the idea. I say idea, when I mean infatuation. That was probably when the idea took shape. *Infatuation.* When we ordered at the restaurant, which was full of people like us, my face burned and the rain dripped out of my hair, and I shook off like a Labrador, and the drops went flying, and Mike laughed, and laughter is one way to shake yourself.

Shaking yourself is the only way to survive. Like an antelope that just barely escapes shakes itself. Like a cat that encounters a handsy child shakes itself. What ails me is grief, I thought. Grief that refuses to be budged. Heavy and unyielding and still, and if I shake myself, then it will move. If I laugh, I shake.

Mike made me laugh. Or maybe I laughed entirely of my own doing. Like every other middle-aged woman in khaki who gets soaked in a downpour giggles. But in my mind, Mike became some kind of remedy, something that could shift all this grief that needed to be shaken apart, once and for all.

It's so strange with discoveries. How little they change anything. Like Hans Christian Andersen's little girl and her matches. A swish and then there's light, a dream, then out. A few more times after that and then done.

Mike ordered massaman curry and a draft beer. I asked for tom kha gai soup and a Krating Daeng. He looked like Marlon Brando, I thought all of a sudden—like a stretched out, unhappy Marlon Brando. He tried to catch my eye, but as soon as he did, he looked away. I asked how he pictured his future. What he thought life would be like in his new house in the sun and sand of Ko Samui.

I picture time passing, slowly and steadily growing old. Living in such a way that I can feel it. Not doing anything. Just breathing. Eating and shitting and breathing.

That answer, I thought, didn't suggest that he'd come to Thailand in order to purchase the services of young women while he drank himself into an early grave, far away from the objections of friends and family.

What are you drinking? he asked and I told him I'd gotten hooked on energy drinks, that I rarely drank coffee and never alcohol. Mike was surprised, and I explained to him why I didn't drink.

It wasn't like me at all. I'm not in the habit of explaining myself to other people. I don't know why I thought Mike a fitting confidant. Can't wrap my head around what it was in his demeanor that awakened those feelings in me, that rapport and that longing for intimacy.

When I was a teenager—sixteen, seventeen, I don't remember precisely— I got drunk for the first and last time. My friend's parents went on a trip abroad, and she and her brother were left at home alone.

We decided to throw a party. Her brother invited his buddies and we invited our girlfriends. Then we drank homebrewed *landi* and beer. We listened to Little Eva, put the needle on "The Loco-Motion" until we scratched the record. I did some shots, drank a beer. There was a discolored reprint of a Matisse painting on the wall, that really famous one where naked women are holding hands and running in a ring on the grass under a blue sky. I hate that painting. *The Dance.*

I hate "The Loco-Motion." Twirling in a circle, kicking with a rustle of skirts out of the arms of brother, into the arms of brother's friend, into the arms of another friend of brother's, back to brother, then black. The next thing I knew, it was tomorrow. My friend was next to me in bed. I was still wearing my skirt, but no tights.

I remember everything.

Acrylic carpet under the soles of my feet.

Remember everything.

Yellow and coarse with streaks of orange.

Remember everything.

The wood-grain pattern in the plastic paneling on the walls in the hallway.

Remember everything.

The moss-green tiles.

Remember everything.

The pictures on the wall.

Remember everything.

Every single thing.

Remember everything.

The colors, the shapes, whether they were originals or reprints.

The porcelain on the shelves.

The white swarm of porcelain children and the little match girl atop a cigarette box:

Help yourself.

I remember everything.

The Danish commemorative plates, one for each year, and which ones were missing.

Remember the sound when the water gushed out of the tap in the sink, into a flimsy cup, into my mouth, parched, and remember how it poured into me and where I stopped feeling it in my throat.

I remember the fibers in my dress, remember them well, and how much I hated them. Don't know why, but I hated them and how they constructed a web that tightened across my breasts and my womb. Where did those fibers come from? Knots of wool or cotton or linen that were spun into thread. Where? Who spun that thread, and what were they thinking when they did it? I hated them. My tights stretched taut between dining room chairs. Paper-thin, sand colored, and bound tightly to the chair feet, threaded between them like a cat's cradle. Never knew why. Never found out. No one remembered. Alcohol poisoning? Second-rate beer or landi or too much of it. In the air, the aggravating stench of bile.

My friend drank the next weekend and her brother, too, and our friends and her brother's friends, but I never drank again.

Not even a sip.

Clever girl, said Mike and raised his glass to me.

When we got back to the guesthouse that night, he invited me to his room. We took off our shoes and lay down side by side in the double bed. Mike opened a beer and we watched television.

A general was holding a press conference. Sitting next to him, the felon, bare chested. Handcuffed and crying. The general spoke slowly and calmly. Described the felony in a deliberate manner and with each word, the felon struggled to hide his face deeper into his chest. Mike groaned. I don't know whether from tiredness or pity.

How do you picture your life in Thailand?

Living in such a way that I can feel myself breathing.

I've always had to pay attention to the small things in order to survive. The outline of a fungus-ridden toenail, visible in a sock. The faintly sweet smell of an oily scalp. Black insect hairs sticking out of ears or noses or birthmarks. These details keep me grounded and remind me who I am—in what body I'm traveling, its boundaries—and they protect me. Hold me at a certain distance, fill me with revulsion and spare me from ideological missteps.

Love. Desire. Longing.

Look at your hands, said my grandma when I was little and was dreading going to scouts or on a field trip or to choir practice or just to school.

Look at your hands and remember who has hands. Who has hands?

Humans have hands.

And who is a human?

I am a human.

My infatuation breaks through these defenses and blinds me. It is, of course, a bit of a trope, I know, but I'm blinded and don't see what is in front of me. Not his face, not his mannerisms, not his expression—I don't understand what it means. It all wipes away before my eyes. Varicose veins, tendons, enlarged pores, blue veins, private skin in crooks, liked sliced cheese. Dark brown urine at the start of the day. Inflamed gums. Erases.

What does he mean?

Inviting me into his bed.

Why doesn't he say anything?

What is he thinking?

Those wrists are perfect.

His scent.

Was it that scent that threw me off balance? Could it have been something so primitive?

I've considered that, in all seriousness. Whether it was something completely animalistic. That something in our unique gene combinations had hit it off so well. I was forty-six years old. It would have been the absolute last chance. I had no desire to have a child, but did my body want one? Speechless, expectant, and having shut off the security system at the worst possible time?

Looking back, there are countless flashing signs. Things he said. Faces he made and the way he moved. By themselves they mean nothing, but when I put all the pieces together, I see perfectly well what he was. Should have seen it the whole time, but when I was lying there beside him, all I wanted was to better feel his warmth.

Come closer, I thought, and I burned, and he burped from the beer without excusing himself.

What did you do before you retired?

I was a truck driver.

Did you like it?

The nomadic life suited me.

What were you transporting?

Oooohhhh, this and that.

Like what?

Corpses. Firearms. Children . . . in bubble wrap.

The theater company received a message from Ellen. She said she didn't feel up to attending more rehearsals because her mom was really ill but that she trusted us completely with her work.

I soon took my leave as well, though I promised to lend the set designer a hand when the time came. Then another message arrived. Ellen said she'd been reading over the play and wanted to ask the whole company, in all seriousness, whether it might not be advisable to postpone the production.

This angered the director. He felt Ellen's behavior showed a lack of respect toward other people's work, and he reminded her that she'd signed a contract. Did she realize the amount of money that had already been dedicated to this project, and that all of that money would go up in smoke if she just up and changed her mind now? More people jumped into the fray. The email thread soon became so long that I lost track of the conversation, but the bottom line was that the play would not be taken off the schedule.

Good luck getting your next play staged, were the director's last words to Ellen and actually, the last word in the argument altogether, because Ellen wrote nothing in reply.

I didn't see her for a few months. I expected to on opening night, but she was nowhere to be seen. The show received mixed reviews. The director, in collaboration with the theater's dramaturge, had, it's true, simplified the story considerably, and they'd cut out almost all of the props I'd been hired to make.

The show was well done—the actors acquitted themselves well, and the set design was good. The script itself was pretty well written, considering the age of the playwright, etc., etc. Then the media got wind of Ellen's dissatisfaction with the production. I suspected that the director himself had a hand in making this news. Ellen didn't respond to any inquiries, and so nothing came of the media circus that the director had no doubt been hoping for.

They kept two props. One was an enormous hole clad with turf roofing on the inside—the hole revolved and narrowed and widened like a spiral down into the stage. The set designer was entirely responsible for this, in collaboration with the props department.

The other sculpture was a giant green boa constrictor. I was responsible for that and made it to the exact specifications of the script. Like it was a real snake. It was sixteen feet long and weighed five hundred and fifty pounds. From the audience, there was no possible way to determine if the snake was real, and not when you got closer to it, either. You had to actually touch it to be certain, but even then, people weren't at ease.

The green boa constrictor was more real than a real snake, if I do say so myself. So real that it slithered around in people's thoughts for the whole of the performance, even though it just lay there, stock-still. All the characters were crushed to death. Some went into the spiral and others into the embrace of the snake. Several critics found this altogether predictable, while others talked about *a play on clichés*.

Personally, I found it beyond satisfying to watch the characters be squeezed and tortured. It's supposed to be strangely comical, but no one laughed. These scenes were long and awkward. The same thing over and over. Some critics talked about repetitiveness, while others talked about *a play on repetition.*

No critic talked about the obvious Freudian connections. How many characters were encircled by death rather than being shot or stabbed. They probably considered such talk outdated and a little cheesy, but in its place, a lot of energy went into the discussion of interactive trickery and Hreiðar's ideological approach.

I regretted not having liked Ellen's play from the start. The fact was, the more often I heard the lines, the better it became. The sentences did an about-face and blazed ever more brightly the more familiar they became. On opening night, I felt the director was wrong, not the play, and I kept thinking about his last words in the email thread:

Good luck getting your next play staged.

And I wondered what effect those words had. Whether some people would understand them to signal the end of their artistic career and whether those people included Ellen. I found it sad. At the same time, I was also mystified by the maternal feelings she aroused in me.

I had never responded to her apology. As a rule, I recoil at even the slightest rejection and instantly forget the person. An apology in a text message was in no way sufficient to heal the wound.

In the interim, I finished all my projects for the Nordic noir picture—the rhino horn, seven chunks of the body of a teenage girl. The head scorched and foam in the mouth, the eyes staring and long-since burst, midterror. A scar on the actress's face. I decided the scar was from acid.

It's fun to create aftereffects of acid. How it dissolves everything, makes puddles out of even the sturdiest molecules.

I made the hand on which a big toe had been grafted in place of the thumb—which was a distinguishing feature of the criminal—and a mink, which had been gutted and filled with drugs. I actually suggested to the director that they find a mink farm and get a few carcasses to freeze, but he shuddered at the thought.

Instead, he wanted me to make an odorless, painless copy. Sometimes I wondered about people's fascination with splatter films and gore, this perpetual need to be revolted. I've fulfilled so many repulsive work requests, and the people who send them to me are so prim. Men in yolk-yellow jeans and women with delicately shaped mouths. It's interesting.

Or maybe not. Maybe it's just utterly, maddeningly uninteresting. The people who carry real horrors within them usually know to be ashamed of themselves. Up and cut their own throats all of a sudden in their sleep, much to everyone's astonishment.

The glass horse was at the bottom of a dresser drawer at home. When I couldn't think of a sufficiently definitive way to destroy it, I threw it in that drawer. Then many weeks passed. Every time I came home, I saw the dresser there in the hallway, thought about the horse, and a wave of pain washed through me.

Now I've grown accustomed to the pain, learned to take it, like every other bitter pill. And so, one afternoon, I opened the drawer, took out the horse, and stuck it in my pocket. Then I went back out, drove a few laps around town. When it got dark, I drove to his house a couple towns over, in Garðabær. I parked not far away. Watched through the kitchen window, which faced the street. Saw his wife busying herself over a pot. Was he going to just sit in the living room watching the news while she cooked cabbage rolls or baked or breaded cod?

Fjóla, his sister and my friend, was dead—had a coronary, then a blood clot, and finally went into cardiac arrest, not but sixty or so. That was when I saw him again. At the funeral, and I saw everything. Remembered everything. Knew everything. It was so strange. First, it was his face, how it had aged, where the wrinkles had formed, then his gaze, how he averted it from my own. The message came in a flash, and I had no doubt, not for one, single second.

What he'd done to me lived on in his cells and his elementary particles and had, in time, become visible.

I'm a loser, his eyes said.

I attack girls while they're sleeping, said his pursed lips.

I'm a necrophiliac, it said on his forehead.

The evening progressed. I saw the shape of him a few times. They went to bed around eleven. Man and wife, in their golden years. I lurked for another hour or so and at midnight, crept up to the house, rifled around in the flowerpot and found the key under it. People are so predictable, so chock-full of trust.

The idea to hide the house key under a mat or in a flowerpot has never crossed my mind. I've never understood why people didn't expect a break-in. Not that I'm so afraid of thieves or in fear for my life, but rather that I expect them and, in some sense, we're always being robbed, every day of our lives. Sometimes of love or happiness, but always, at the very least, of truth.

The door opened without a sound, and I edged my way in like a shadow. Closed it gently behind me and crept into the hall, saw the same kind of dresser that I have at home myself. There was a little screech when I opened the top drawer. I held my breath, stood stock-still. There were gloves and scarves in the drawer.

All things that belong to his wife, I thought to myself, and how appropriate it would be to leave her the horse. I put it at the very top. Right atop a blue kerchief.

Just so.

Then I went out again. Closed the door behind me without a sound and stuck the key under the flowerpot.

A horse made of scarves—dowdy, beige, blue, patterned, polyester, and, occasionally, silk scarves—broke into a gallop, took off into the night, and disappeared.

Lilja said Ellen got her impetuousness from her dad, who had been too impetuous for this world.

Am I too impetuous for this world? Ellen asked once when she was little, and Lilja said that neither she nor her daughter was of this world, they weren't made for this world, weren't made of the same stuff as the world.

It's trolls, she said, trolls who built this country. They used their wiles to escape the sun, and now, everything turns to stone.

Lilja was on the phone when she came in. Ellen stopped and listened for a moment.

. . . The cemetery is open to everyone, she said.

. . . Anyone is free to leave flowers for anyone.

. . . Or wool, or just whatever they want.

. . . It's perfectly permissible to dig into the soil a little . . . such as for flower bulbs.

My daughter wants to talk to you, she then said suddenly and handed Ellen the phone.

Tell them it's a work of art, she whispered as Ellen took the phone.

It wasn't the first time the police had been in touch over what Álfur Finnsson's widow called acts of graveyard vandalism. Lilja called them installations or sculptures or "Ephemeral Monuments" or "Of Loss YR I, II, and III" or "Footsteps From Inside a Woman" or most recently, "WARM SILENCE!"

She had stuck tent pegs into the dirt on Álfur's grave and used them to trace the shape of a sweater and then wove the yarn from his old sweater between the pegs, close and tight.

The cemetery caretaker was friendly. He asked how Ellen was doing and said this was just a reminder. He was apologetic when he said that the widow, Laufey, had mentioned something about the police and a restraining order. Ellen promised to try and talk to her mom but noted that her mother did have a right to visit the grave of her child's father.

Visit, yes, said the caretaker. It's just this thing with the tent pegs and the yarn that's crossed the line.

I understand, said Ellen, looking into the expectant eyes of her mother.

But I hope you understand as well that my mother is an artist, and this is the way she expresses herself, that she's doing this out of respect for my father's memory.

Of course, said the caretaker, and hung up. Lilja took her phone back and showed Ellen the photos she'd taken of the grave with the yarn stretched taut across it.

It makes you want to lie down in those outstretched arms, said Ellen, and her mom nodded. She lit a cigarette without even noticing and asked Ellen how it'd gone at the theater. But before she'd gotten an answer, Lilja received a notification on her phone about a new email, which she then read aloud.

It was a rejection letter from the Reykjavík Art Museum. A few months earlier, Lilja had submitted an application to hold a show in one of the small galleries. Ellen had stayed up all night with her and helped her put together the application. Her mom had had a very clear idea for the show, and they were happy with the file they'd ended up sending to the museum.

Why did they say no? Lilja interrupted herself in the middle of reading. They don't say anything at all. Just some please try again at a later time blah blah blah.

Ellen looked over her mother's shoulder and skimmed the short letter.

Should we call? asked Lilja, but Ellen said it wouldn't do any good.

And they're surprised I sneak into the cemetery at night. There's no space for me anywhere! I'm suffocating!

Did you sleep last night? asked Ellen, letting her mother's histrionics pass without comment.

Maybe a little, I don't know. I don't remember.

Should I call the doctor?

Ugh, no.

Ellen went into her room and closed the door behind her while she got the key to the medicine cabinet. The medicine cabinet was in the broom closet in the kitchen, a white steel box with a green cross on the front. She found the right pills and locked the cabinet immediately, then filled a glass from the tap and gave her mom her medicine. She swallowed them all at once.

Over and out, Lilja mumbled and sat in her chair next to the yellow table, lit a cigarette, and looked blankly out over the bay.

That's better, she murmured, and Ellen went into her bedroom. The blackout curtains were still pulled across the window, but instead of opening them, she turned on the light. She let herself fall back onto her twin-size kid's bed, which she didn't even notice was uncomfortable, and yanked the script out of her bag.

As far as she could remember, her bedroom had never been painted, and Ellen had lived in it as long as she could remember. There was a piece of art on the wall that her mother had made when she was at the Arts Academy. It was the word *VOID* written with tar on a faded billboard, smeared under glass, and carefully framed.

The walls of her room were, like the other walls of the apartment, covered with scribbles and drawings. From the moment she'd learned to wield a crayon, her mom had encouraged her to draw on anything she laid eyes on and, sometimes, they drew on the walls.

At some point, one of Ellen's classmates figured out that at her house, you could draw on the wall and cut up the furniture if you felt like it would serve an artistic purpose, and after that the walls were also covered with drawings by any and every kid in the neighborhood.

Still, it was only one boy who cut up the couch. He had frantically scrawled on the door and had started to make animal noises, jumped between the furniture and then went into the kitchen and came back out armed with a kitchen knife that he stabbed to the hilt and pulled out of the Chesterfield sofa.

Lilja observed the boy composedly as he froze and his eyes widened, looked at the knife in his little hand and the stab wound in the leather. He was a sorry sight.

There, now, said Lilja, producing a colorful pocket scarf that she stuck into the wound.

That's nice, she said, patting the boy on the cheek. The wound was still there, but not the scarf.

One time, a girl came over after school. Ellen was eleven years old. The girl was in the grade above her and Ellen was a little afraid of her, and also a little full of herself, what with the girl coming for a visit. Ellen recognized that the girl was from another world. You could see on her skin and in the whites of her eyes that she was just stopping over in Ellen and Lilja's reality for a short time.

Lilja greeted her and asked if they wanted something to drink or eat. Would they like some coffee?

I don't drink coffee! protested Ellen, and the girl giggled. She didn't drink coffee either.

Then may I offer you girls soda or tea . . . or water?

The Coke's flat, said Ellen warningly. We've had it since New Year's. The girl giggled and said that she wasn't thirsty. She was looking at everything in the apartment as if she had paid admission. She was a head taller than Ellen and had long black hair that was all wavy and shiny. Under her white sweater were breasts that Ellen had once seen in the shower after swim class and knew were shaped like pyramids.

She also knew that those breasts were significant. That the shine in her hair was significant, but she didn't entirely understand why it mattered so much to her, Ellen. When they'd spoken for the first time in the schoolyard the day before and the girl was friendly, Ellen knew all too well that the other shoe would drop, that the girl wasn't chatting just to chat. Girls like that don't do anything just because.

The hope was still there, though, fledgling and bright in Ellen's flat chest, the hope that the first day in a new life was now upon her. She wasn't entirely sure what this life would be like, but she could smell it in the girl's hair, heard the merriment in her percussive laughter.

Doesn't your mom ever clean? whispered the girl adoringly when they were in Ellen's room, and Ellen was suddenly aware of the state of her home. Regretted having let the girl come over, but at the same time, knew it was the only option. Because the only reason the girl was interested was the stories that went around about Ellen and her mom and all the odd goings-on at their house.

So what's it really like to have a mom who's so mental? asked the girl. There was genuine curiosity in her voice. With her intonation, the word *mental* became a compliment.

Ellen didn't answer. She turned on her computer and was going to find a funny video that she'd seen the night before and show the girl.

Yeah, I've seen it, said the girl impatiently, opening a dresser drawer.

Don't open my drawers! yelped Ellen, slamming it shut again.

Sorry! giggled the girl, and Ellen got embarrassed. She wanted the girl to leave, but she couldn't say that. She suggested that they go to the corner store, but the girl just made a face.

What do your parents do? asked Ellen, and the girl said her dad was in politics and her mom worked as the manager of an athletic association. She reeled off the words without the slightest bit of interest, and Ellen decided not to ask anything else.

Is it true that you can just destroy anything here? asked the girl suddenly, and Ellen saw the spark of something in her eyes, something so aggressive that she looked away.

No, of course not, she answered quickly.

But everyone says you can, said the girl disappointedly. She looked around at the scribbles on the dingy walls, the naked wall sockets and all the clutter.

I can't even write something on the wall? she asked.

No, said Ellen.

Can I go to the bathroom, then? she asked, and Ellen said she could go to the bathroom, but then she had to leave.

The girl went out and Ellen sat in her room, took her pillow in her arms, and lifted it up to her face. Shortly after, she heard her mother's laughter blending with the girl's tinkling voice. She went out and saw that the girl was drawing on the living room wall. She was just scribbling anything with a black permanent marker, neither words nor pictures, just scribbling like an idiot, and Ellen stopped in the doorway, leaned on the wall, and observed the girl and Lilja.

They laughed, and the girl scrawled, and Lilja said something and turned on the radio, and it was some jazz program and a trumpet solo, and the girl had enough of scribbling on the wall. She got on her knees and scribbled on the parquet floor.

No one had scribbled on the parquet before.

Not the floor! yelped Ellen, but her mother just smiled at her, and the girl scribbled, swung her shining hair and scuttled across the floor and scribbled.

Like a spider that scuttled around leaving black lines in its wake, and Ellen grabbed her white sweater, wrenched her to her feet.

Tsk tsk, said Lilja, standing between them. Don't interfere with her self-expression, she said blandly.

She's ruining the floor! Ellen protested.

The floor is just a floor; it's dead, just a thing. Your friend and her self-expression are life itself, right now, this moment, much more important . . . Ellen yanked the marker out of the girl's hand and waggled it across her sweater, leaving a black line on her pyramid breasts. The girl was aghast.

Are you retarded? asked the girl. Ellen waggled the marker again, left a black line across her stomach. The girl backed away.

You're both mental, she said and lurched into the hallway, slamming the door behind her without saying goodbye.

Lilja put her hand over her mouth. She laughed. That was fun, she said. You should invite your friends over more often.

The young one showed up at the same time that Lilja got sick. Ellen never saw the child with her own eyes. Nor the old one who'd rampaged around the apartment, impossible to keep in check. The old one's hair fell heavily, gray and lank, arms swinging like a punch-drunk gorilla, grunting with rage. Spewing words that were unlistenable in their ugliness, the young one slipping out of sight.

Ellen saw neither the young one nor the old one and, consequently, she would not talk about them or answer them out loud, but she lived with them nevertheless, as did Lilja. When she first became aware of the young one, they were the same age—six or seven years old. Then Ellen turned eight, nine, ten years old. But the young one was never more than seven.

The young one could be really mean and was always competing with Ellen. Seized her rights from her. You have no right to this or that, Ellen was told, and if she made a mistake, the kid could turn cruel.

That's just like you, said the kid. Lilja hugged Ellen and said everyone made mistakes. *You can't do anything right,* came the whisper then, and Ellen would get scared that the old one would come running in and would hit her in the head with a wooden spoon.

The old one was physically violent on occasion, and sometimes at night, Ellen would jerk awake with the fear that the house was being set on fire, a pillow being held over her face.

Lilja went out of focus, slowed all her movements, hardly enunciated any of her words. Ellen left her in peace, tried to ignore the viciousness, pretended not to hear the tumult of the old one.

Then one day, Ellen suggested they go for just a short walk. Lilja made a face. The day after, she suggested a very short walk once more and the day after, too, until, in the end, Lilja agreed. Ellen took care that they went out just as the sun was at its highest so that Lilja would get some light. Her skin was completely bloodless and matte. Her eyes irritated. They threaded their arms together as those paupers, the young one and the old one, trailed behind them, poorly dressed, forlorn, and exhausting.

Lilja's doctor was mostly in touch with Ellen. He had a deep, soothing voice, and she liked it when he said things like *we'll see how it goes* and *tomorrow is another day*. The words had no meaning, no purpose other than to emphasize the inadequacy of medical science when faced with the inner workings of Lilja's brain, but all the same, they made Ellen feel like she wasn't alone in the world when he was mumbling them over the phone.

After one such phone call, she remembered me. She got a twinge in her stomach and wrote me two text messages:

I didn't meat to be a cunt

and:

mean

She expected that I'd send an answer in return, and then she planned to ask me to meet her because she needed advice on the script. But I didn't answer and consequently, she didn't dare ask me about anything. She also regretted having used the word *cunt*. First *lesbo* and then *cunt*. So crass!

You don't say words like that to women of a respectable age, she thought, her earlobes blushing as she did. When I think that she should have felt ashamed of herself because of me, blushed because of me, the corners of my mouth turn up, just a little, and my eyes get a little watery and my throat constricts ever so slightly. My stomach hot, all of a sudden.

Sweet girl.

Someone was inside. I could feel it the moment I opened my front door. It was two o'clock in the morning. I had stopped off at a market that's open all night and was carrying a bag of groceries.

Hallö? I called and stood there quietly for a long time in the semi-darkness. I could see the faint gleam of a light in the living room that I could have very well left on myself. No one answered. Slowly and calmly, I headed for the living room where I knew he was waiting for me—the pale man. He was wearing neither a coat nor mittens. He sat sprawled there on the floor, dressed in a black band T-shirt. The name of the band told me nothing at all, but under it, there were dates from the summer of '87.

He looked into my eyes, expressionless, nodded his head slightly. He'd laid out three things in front of him. On his left was a spherical wig, a sort of hairy ball. On his right, there was some strange leather pouch, as if it were many centuries old, brittle and foul smelling. Right in front of him was the plant. The one I'd found behind the TV.

Tillandsia, isn't it? I said, and I wondered how in the world I could have forgotten this discovery, this exotic air plant behind my television.

The fact remains, and this is maybe the only thing I've truly learned from my time here on earth, that it is precisely the main points that pass—should I say *US?*—by. No. They pass me by. The details, clearer than I care for, appear before me all day, all the way down to their atoms, but the main points I forget like a shot.

You don't remember me, said the man quietly. His voice like flapping wings and I said, yes, I remembered very well when he came and picked up my boxes. Then I wanted to know who he was and why he was brooding about my personal matters, breaking in and leaving behind old things in new places.

He turned bashful and didn't say a thing. He'd trudged in without taking off his shoes, mucky clogs that had left a trail of mud in their wake. Instead, he lifted the wig ball and the leather pouch and swapped them back and forth a few times, as if he intended to do a magic trick. Every time he lifted these things, I got a small pain in my stomach, but I said nothing and I did nothing.

The man overflowed like water and it was all too late before it happened. I didn't even try to find an explanation. I was old enough to know that in most instances, they were entirely lacking and I didn't feel like expending the energy to search for something that didn't exist.

How come the police are searching for you? I asked instead, and the man's expression almost changed. Or else his face was as petrified as before, but his head twitched ever so slightly.

How old are you? I asked.

Fifty-nine, he said and looked into my eyes again, and it wasn't until then that I saw something familiar in them. As he got to his feet and took slow steps back out of the living room, I didn't look away until he'd vanished. I didn't hear the door, but I knew he was long gone.

Grandma was the wig master and worked in the sewing room at the theater. She sat there in the basement, weaving human hair all the live-long day, a focused expression on her face. That profession brought her great satisfaction, although she didn't take any particular pleasure from the theater. Sometimes, we went to opening night together and then Grandma said we were going to see the wigs.

I always felt a little uncomfortable in a theater. It seemed strange to see people moving and speaking in such a performative way. Like catching someone in a lie. Then it would happen every so often that the script would move me, and I'd hear what the actors said—feel, even, that they were talking to me.

After one such performance, I described my experience, and Grandma said that that was the mark of a high-quality show—it got you to forget yourself.

Just think, she said, that's what we humans are always striving for— to forget ourselves and to let ourselves be forgotten. That's what it's all about.

Forget what? I asked.

It is so dreadfully painful to be human, explained Grandma, and sometimes, the only way to bear it is to forget. I forget myself over my wigs—they're such top quality—didn't you think they looked fine tonight? Did you see the sweep across the lieutenant's forehead?

Yes, I answered, recalling the red-gold mane on the villain of the play, how it shone and undulated in the mellow stage lights.

They'd just managed to pay off the house before Grandpa died in an accident. If he'd died a few months before, your mom would've been made a ward of the parish and sent into foster care out in the country-side, Grandma sometimes said, and it always made me shudder. The Parish. It sounded like something that crunched children between its teeth. Grandma sewed all day, all night—men's suits, confirmation gowns, stitched goldwork onto national costumes. Her hardanger embroidery was so beautiful on the reverse side that people got con-fused. Thus she managed to keep the house and body and soul together, so that her child wasn't made a ward of the parish, even if almost all her family was dead.

Women in our family, Grandma sometimes said, they might glide by sight unseen, but they make it all the same. Then she got a position at the theater. She made wigs that she hung up all over at home and that were so real they could have just as easily been scalps she'd collected. She worked at the theater during the day, but in the evenings she sat in the living room with pins between her lips, threading strands of hair that were so fine as to be invisible.

Your grandpa was the most engaging man in the world, the funniest, the best man you could think up, Grandma said once. He two-timed me and drank his every waking moment, but I was so sweet on him, and I thought myself lucky to have him. And, of course, we had your mom.

Then once, when he was drunk, he fell out a window—not even a particularly long way down, but still long enough to break his neck, and it was as if I'd broken my neck, too, said Grandma. As if all the conduits to my brain had been severed, and I don't remember a thing. We had no help and your poor mother.

One Christmas, it rolled out of a gift box—the hairball. She'd made a wig and sewn it onto a rubber ball, about the size of a softball, but heavier and full of liquid. I turned it over in my hands and shuddered instinctively. It was my hair.

What am I supposed to do with this? I asked Grandma, who just laughed her husky laugh.

I don't know if anyone thought my dad was the most engaging man in the world. It's more than likely that Mom didn't, since she neither spoke nor understood English. But I'm sure she thought he was handsome in his uniform and so tall in his shiny boots. With the kind of foreign allure that you could bottle up and sell.

Still, I don't know. No one knows. Grandma thought she'd eventually say who my dad was, but then she was dead and left nothing behind except for a tiny babe that didn't know a thing. Grandma was nearly fifty then. She imagined that my dad had been an American soldier, imagined dances and infatuation and heady interludes, but I've always had my doubts.

Mom lived with Grandma. In the bedroom that later became my bedroom, which was in the apartment that was sold at the beginning of this story. She worked in the costumes department with Grandma and had just turned twenty-two. Her sweetheart had dumped her, found someone new, and she was completely devastated.

She'd taken to drinking a bit, Grandma sometimes said.

Grandma was worried and wanted Mom to go into service in the countryside. Mom wouldn't hear of it. Mom said that life was so pointless, it wasn't worth it. Before you know it, I'll have had five kids with someone I despise, with someone who despises me, and then I'll cease to exist, she said, then I'll become a cog in my sewing machine and repeat myself for all eternity.

She'd taken to reading a bit, Grandma sometimes said.

Grandma noticed the change. They were close, Grandma often said. She clearly sensed that Mom wasn't herself, but didn't figure out what was going on until Mom was halfway through her pregnancy. Then she refused to get out of bed.

My friend Fjóla was more curious about my dad than I was. She wanted to know whether Grandma had any leads.

Did Mom go to balls with soldiers?

Without a doubt.

Was that where I was conceived, at a ball with soldiers or in a Nissen hut full of soldiers or in an alley with a soldier? Was Dad wearing a uniform when the embryo anchored itself securely in her uterine lining, bored its way in? Was he wearing boots—how tall, how shiny? Was he carrying a gun? Did he smell of faraway places, did he smell like oil, denim, cotton bolls, yellow straw, engines, Juicy Fruit, rum and Coke, Camels?

Did it smell like it does under a car? Did she see movies flickering behind her eyes, a woman coming down a flight of stairs in a floor-length, custom-made gown, no one knows what color, ready for the ball?

An accidental discharge.

Regardless of whether he was a soldier or not.

Mama died suddenly. I was too little to remember her. When I was a teenager, I occasionally pestered Grandma, wanted to know all the particulars, but sensed that it was overwhelming for her. She mentioned pills, vodka, said I hadn't been aware of anything.

After my mom died, Grandma tried to find my dad. She asked former sweethearts, girlfriends, bartenders, soldiers. She walked around with a photograph of Mom in her wallet and took it out whenever she found a reason to.

When I got older and became curious, she told me that no one knew who my dad was. He himself had no idea I existed, but if he ever found out, he'd naturally be overjoyed to have such a well-behaved girl like me.

I look like him. No one has ever said it, but I don't look anything like Mom. My face looks like the face of a man who no one knows or knows what became of. My mannerisms those of a man who has no idea that I exist.

Most often when police put out missing-person alerts, they are for teens who people figure will end up being found at some party or just hanging around. Somewhere in a heap of other lost teens trying to get even more lost.

If the missing person is older, you suspect that they've walked into the sea or committed a crime or been murdered. Sometimes, you'll see an announcement a few days later that they've turned up again. Sometimes not.

I've often thought about disappearing myself, but only when I've been certain that someone would notice. When I was a child, I plotted my escape. Pictured bare toes on a bright gravel road, endless sunshine, and good-hearted people who would give me soup and bread and let me sleep in their hayloft.

When I was a young woman, I pictured an inexpensive hotel room in a city where I didn't understand a single, solitary word of the language. I pictured bottles of liquor and people who came and went. A new life that began far away from this old one, getting to become someone else.

There are so many ways to disappear. When I've been at my lowest, I've thought about how I could vanish without a trace. I didn't want it to end with someone stumbling upon my body at the edge of a forest. A rowboat out in an open sea of sleeplessness and a shotgun report.

Still, the most common, most unostentatious disappearances take place within a person. When the personality takes over the work of the soul and continues onward, fully mechanized, with the help of the body.

There were, perhaps, only a few people who took note when I went to Thailand, but I met Mike, who was a missing person himself—not because he was missed, per se, but because he had to be stopped.

I put off my trip to Kuala Lumpur, and Mike and I went sightseeing around Bangkok. In the evenings, we ate exotic dishes that amount to little more in my memory than insects and shrimp and nuts and deep-fried finger food. We'd sit silently, side by side in the ferry that sailed between the different parts of town, and I'd close my eyes, feel exactly where his thigh was, where his hand rested, my breast aching with desire.

Then we'd go back to the hotel and sometimes he'd invite me to his room, but most of the time we'd just say goodnight. I didn't know what the thing I longed for was supposed to be like. Couldn't imagine it. That all of a sudden, I'd lean my head toward him, wait for a kiss? Or lay myself in his arms, and just wait there, just on the off chance? What if he pushed me away? I wasn't sure I could bear that. And so I didn't do anything, and neither did he.

As soon as we went our separate ways, my head filled with questions. I didn't understand what he wanted from me and went over all of our interactions ad nauseam until every minuscule detail, pause between words, slip of the tongue, became significant and revealing. I got confused. I have never been as confused as I was when I was with Mike. Even the woman in the mirror seemed transformed. Her expression that of someone who is about to get off. Pathetic.

Whether he knew. Wanted. What he wanted. What did Mike want? the woman with the orgasmic expression was always asking. So mortifying. If this had been after the arrival of the internet, I could have typed in his name and seen exactly what he wanted, but there was no internet. Just postal mail and undecipherable daily papers in Thai and others in English that were sold in special bookstores I never went to.

So it was that I sat in my room, murdering mosquitoes, splatter on the wall, and wondering.

What does he want?

Not me.

Except maybe in chunks.

If he felt like it.

One day, I didn't see him at breakfast like usual. The night before, he'd said he was tired and we hadn't gone out like we'd planned. I went to his room and knocked on the door. Heard someone moving around, but no one came to the door. There was a lizard that lived in the hallway that I stared at, spellbound. Its throat bulged out, a bright red balloon that looked like it was bursting, then snapped back into its throat again.

I had to show Mike. What was I thinking? I knocked again. I'm not used to being so close with other people. Still am not entirely sure of the rules. He yanked the door open. His eyes were oddly protuberant, and he shouted something. I couldn't make out anything he said, froze. He slammed the door in my face.

Was there someone in his room? I wasn't sure, and yet, I felt like I'd made out some animate thing. A shadow that stirred.

People sometimes sought out my company. People who wanted to be my associates, friends even, and over time, I noticed something. These people had something in common.

I had a type.

The Type never arrived empty-handed. Was always wanting to foist gifts off on me. Later, I'd always find something wrong with the gifts. If it was something to eat, it had expired; if it was clothing, it didn't fit at all. This usually ended with me unburdening myself of them—throwing the food in the trash or taking the garments to a donation bin, which was a tedious hassle.

Once The Type had presented their gift, they'd want to have a coffee and sit in my breakfast nook and talk. They'd talk without pausing for breath and tell me far more than I cared to know. They'd talk about themselves and the people in their lives, and I never believed a word they said. There was something about how The Type squinted and lied about the most mundane things. Some dent in the shape of their mouths.

The Type had found themselves in the shit and bore no responsibility for any of it. People had treated The Type so badly that it was as if the world they lived in was composed of shadows. When in the end, they left, they took something with them that I didn't want to give, but it was invisible and irrevocable.

Women and men who came into my life and pressed their palms into my back amid their leapfrog through other people's lives.

I'm silent.

They speak.

I tire.

They feed.

All the stories I've been told. All the confidences I've been made privy to. All the gifts I've been given. I never wanted to get to know The Type.

The Type just came and was and then left in the end. Meanwhile, the people I wanted to get to know were far beyond my reach.

It's not exactly so dramatic, of course, and, of course, there are exceptions. Like Fjóla, who had a brother. She and I kept in touch all the way up until she died, which came as a shock. Sometimes, I simplify things for the sake of the story.

I always started from the assumption that people told lies. I kept an account of betrayals, avoided intimacy, and permitted myself no fantasies, which are, of course, the basis for all relationships.

Until I got to know Mike. He never told me much about himself, and yet, he sought out my company. He didn't ask about anything, either, and maybe it was precisely this silence that led to me starting to entrust him with various things I wasn't accustomed to saying out loud.

Like the story of the glass horse.

Fjóla had a mom who worked and a dad who was often in a good mood and a brother who teased me when I went over to their house. I thought he was cute. She had dozens of cousins who were always coming over without calling ahead. The front door was usually unlocked, and when I went to her house after dinner, we sat in the living room with her mom and dad, who talked to me as if I were an adult.

Fjóla and I were in the same class in our first year of high school, and her mom said we should focus on our studies and not chase after a future husband. They asked what I wanted to do, and I said I wasn't sure that higher education was for me. Grandma was dead set on it, said that it was what Mom would have wanted, but I wasn't sure. I was bored.

They didn't react by urging me to do great things, but rather tried to get at what it was that I wanted to do. What my interests were. This made me self-conscious—I was afraid I'd say something stupid or that I had something between my teeth or hanging out of my nose, or that I smelled bad.

Fjóla just thought her parents were squares. When her dad told jokes, she would roll her eyes furtively, and when her mom criticized the way she dressed, she complained bitterly. She said her mom was too critical, called her dad a moron. I wanted to be her sister, their daughter, or even better: her. I never would have rolled my eyes or complained.

I would have gladly laughed at his jokes, would have paid attention to her comments. I would have dressed the way Mom wanted. I would not miss me.

That's what I thought, at any rate. Her brother was a few years older. He had a job somewhere. Fjóla wasn't overly fond of her brother either, and whenever I asked about him, she was quick to change the subject. I was definitely not the first friend of hers to have a crush on him. He was like that. But I was, perhaps, the first to have such a crush on the whole family. I wanted them to adopt me. Whenever I visited their house, I didn't want to leave. I drank up all the details, all the smells. Their knickknacks, the titles of their books, the state of their plants, everything.

When I think about it now, I'm pretty sure that Fjóla's parents felt sorry for me. At the time, I didn't quite realize that I was dogged by sorrow. In our small community, stories went around that were so tragic, they ended with an orphan living with her eccentric single grandma. It's probable that the parents of all the kids I played with felt sorry for me. Maybe I didn't know any different. But at Fjóla's house, my forsakenness reached a new level, and sometimes I was worried that I'd accidentally say something, just blurt out:

You can have me.

I was, of course, far too old to be acting like that. Sixteen years old and I should have been chasing boys and thinking about how long or tight my skirt was or what someone said to someone else about something. But such frivolity is built on a steady foundation that I lacked. Grandma was getting stranger every day. I suspected that there was something serious going on, but I couldn't follow such thoughts through to their ends.

Fjóla got a crush on her brother's friend. He had a job unloading fish at the harbor and was almost six five. Suddenly, we were meeting up with her brother and his friend on the weekends. They invited us to a party and Fjóla started kissing the tall guy, and her brother looked at me curiously, as if he were trying to figure out if I was worth the trouble. I longed to kiss his family, and by extension, him.

Then his parents went to a summer cottage with friends, and the siblings were left home alone. I drank for the first and last time and then a few weeks later, started getting terrible pains.

Like period cramps, but much worse. If things had been at all normal, I would have complained, but I said nothing. I have a strange memory of standing in the fishmonger's. One of Grandma's friends is asking me how we've been, what's been going on, but I hardly understand a word she's saying because it's taking all my concentration to keep my composure. My face is on the verge of sliding into a painful grimace and I'm sweating at my temples just trying to keep it together.

You're looking a bit pale, said the woman, and I said goodbye. A few days later, I passed out in my bedroom. I came to in the hospital with antibiotics and morphine running through my veins. There was a glass horse on the bedside table. I had never seen it before. There was also a bouquet of flowers, bluebells that I recognized from our garden at home.

The doctor came in. Tall and squishy all over and ogreish with hairy sideburns and small, affectionate eyes. He asked how I felt. I remember that with him there was a nurse, on the older side. It seems to me she had a fatigued expression, more tired than scandalized. I don't remember well enough. Her horn-rimmed glasses are still completely clear in my mind. The mind decides what it thinks is important.

The glass horse seems minuscule in the doctor's hands. His nails are clipped close, yellow from smoking, and his fingers are stumpy. He fiddles with the horse and tries to put something into words but seems to have trouble finding the right ones.

Do you recognize this horse? he asks cautiously at last, and I shake my head.

We found it in your vagina, he says and averts his eyes.

I don't understand what he's saying. The first thing that occurs to me is that the horse came into being in my vagina.

What? I say at last and I remember horn-rims, but not whether anyone laid their hand over mine. Probably not.

Do you have any idea how it got there? asks the doctor and then, all of a sudden, I remember the horse. Remember the knickknack shelves at my friend Fjóla's house and her mom's collection of little glass animals. Remember the horse on one of those shelves.

I shake my head. I want to ask about the pain, about what is being pumped into my veins, but my mouth won't open.

The infection spread to your uterus, but you're getting penicillin and morphine for the pain, says the doctor.

Have you been sexually active for long? he then asks, looking down at his papers.

I'm not, I said.

I've never.

He assumed I was lying.

Mike listened. I wasn't expecting any particular reaction. I just had a funny feeling for a moment. I didn't feel any kind of relief in talking about it, not like a cork from a bottle or a horse from a vagina.

Back in the US, I once took on a small job at this ranch in the woods in the South, said Mike, and there was a farmer there who told me that trees use their roots to talk to each other, down in the earth. When they sense a threat, they warn each other.

But they can't get away . . . I interrupted him.

They release seeds, explained Mike, but I didn't understand what he was talking about. Understood that the survival of the species is paramount for all living things but didn't know why he thought that story applied. I sat up in bed, swung my legs over the edge, caught sight of a lock of hair in the corner.

There are so many kinds of trauma. That one was, in many ways, the most significant one, but how do I explain it? It's complicated. Why did I see that lock of hair at the very moment I'd opened myself up for the first time about what had happened to me as a teenager? Why had I said nothing? Said nothing while the glass dilated, hot at first, then hard, cold, paper-thin, and broken at last.

But I've no part in this trauma. This trauma belongs to the woman whose hair that was. To everyone who loved the woman whose hair that was.

There were tiles on the floor. White and shiny. The bed was in the middle of the room, and on either side of it there were bedside tables made of imitation oak with lions' feet. The lock of hair was under one of these—long, black, and attached to a little swatch of skin.

It's too bad that happened to you, said Mike, stretching out on the bed.

Would you like me to hold you? he asked, which was exactly what I wanted more than anything in the world to hear.

I don't feel well, I managed to stammer. It took a lot out of me to recall that, I added by way of explanation, walking out of the room as slowly as I possibly could. My heart pounded and my blood boiled. To this day, I still have trouble with that kind of tile. Big, shiny, snow-white tiles. Some people's teeth remind me of those tiles, and I have trouble with people who have those kind of teeth. It was only a question of when he'd see the lock of hair that he'd clearly overlooked.

A few days later, there was an accident in Bangkok. A gas explosion on New Petchburi Road. Ninety people lost their lives; one hundred and forty were injured. Then I saw his picture in the paper. Thai script unreadable all around it. I went to a bookstore and bought the most recent papers from America, but there wasn't anything. The news didn't make it over there right away. I had to wait a few days, and, in the meantime, I looked at Mike's face in among the script. His face closed, his eyes dead, black height lines on the white wall behind him. An American mug shot but without the profile. I longed to see his profile. His profile when he was lying down and smiled, the folds of his cheeks, the curve of his nose. I longed for his warmth, his smell.

"The Headhunter's Head" was the title of the article I finally found in a tabloid. It was accompanied by another photo of Mike, in which he was a young man. His hair was slicked back and the lapels of his uniform glinted. His expression open, innocent. He was beautiful, I still think, when I remember him. I still long for something I can't put my finger on when I think about Mike.

> *Michael Howard worked as an archivist at the State Ar-*
> *chives of North Carolina. He was a solemn loner with*
> *few friends. Several months ago, the head of a young*

woman was found in a storage unit that had been rented under a pseudonym. The police followed a trail of clues back to Mr. Howard, who vigorously denied his guilt. Not long after, he disappeared into thin air. . . . The police found a second head, which in this case, had been gibbeted in the middle of nowhere. The women had various things in common—body type, hair color, age. They were both right around twenty years old. Interpol issued a warrant for Michael Howard. It was as if he had never existed. His apartment was so impersonal that it wasn't feasible for investigators to come up with any theories about where he'd gone. . . . Then there was a gas explosion on New Petchburi Road in Bangkok and his head was found, completely undamaged. Authorities were able to identify him using dental records, and thus was the Headhunter run to ground.

Time slowed down, such that all sounds deepened. The April sun shone through the windows, and I could picture my apartment, motes of dust scintillating in the air. My things would die with me. Without me, they were foreign, unfamiliar. No one would pick up this faded, flower-patterned pitcher and think of me.

Some anonymous civil servants would come and pile my things in a dumpster and from there, they'd be taken to the charity shop. They'd be dispersed among the homes of people who had no idea about me or the life I'd had with my pitcher, my tablecloth, my plate, my fork, my spoon, my bowl.

Books. Knickknacks from the Far East. Curtains redolent of tobacco. Ashtrays of colored glass. Raffia baskets. Pots, pans, flower vases, and dented tin boxes.

A speck of my soul must reside in each of these things. It couldn't all just be inanimate stuff. These specks would tag along to the charity shop, go home with people. People who would then drink them out of my cups and piss them into their toilet bowls. They'd be washed up with the dishes and then flow down through the plumbing. The specks so alive and so close. These specks of me on earth after I die. First in people's innards and then in their pipes!

My bedding had gotten shabby. Thin and worn from use. I'd long been on the verge of going to the store to buy a new set, but shrunk from the prospect, found little more depressing than the light in those airplane hangars that sold bedclothes. The bright light, the ceiling height, the legions of people, and the smell of plastic. Landfills come to mind, filled with this junk that was bought in the name of thriftiness and then not used more than twice.

I drove to the outskirts of town, out to one of those enormous warehouses where all such sundries were to be found. Hundreds of duvet covers to choose from. I wanted to sleep under a rustling new one. The patterns were so garish, lurid, nauseating. Vulgarly fashionable designer knockoffs. In the end, I found woven linen bedding that cost twice as much as the others. Beige, coarse, and befitting.

The store was like a maze—pathways led you along in such a way that no allurement escaped your notice. I finally made it to the restaurant and decided to get a cup of coffee and an open-faced sandwich with smoked salmon before I drove back.

In front of me in line was a woman whose back was turned to me. Her hair golden and damp and smelling of shampoo, and she had two little boys with her who were pointing and whining. She looked at me and an earnest smile burst onto her face.

Elín! she said, embracing me. We should have carpooled, she added with a laugh. Did you find your bedding? she asked, but I couldn't place her. How did she know I was buying bedding? She couldn't see it in the yellow bag I was using for a shopping basket.

Don't you recognize me? she asked, and I stared at her face. It's me, *Helen* . . . she whispered, and her smile disappeared. She squeezed my shoulder, shook me a little, as if to offer me support, and the next thing I knew, she was seeing to her boys, ordering them meatballs and telling them they couldn't have soda, cracking jokes, looking at me, laughing. Apologetically. Sadly.

Who was she?
How did she know what I needed?
What did she have to be sad about?

The open-faced sandwiches lay there in the cooler and I looked at the garnishes—rings of bell pepper and a wad of parsley. The pink salmon. I felt queasy. I longed to never have to eat again. Just the thought of getting the food through my body and out again. It seemed like way too much trouble.

In order to get out of the store, I had to thread my way through the entire maze again, but when I reached the beginning, I was directed to go back the way I came. I tried to keep my composure, walked past the living rooms, the bathrooms, and the kitchens and waited in line at the cash register.

I didn't disappear, rather got bigger in this enormous, disinterested space. The faces contorted in my head, blurred together with my own face. *To lose your wits, fall apart, have a nervous breakdown*—these are the privileges of those who have loved ones. I waited in line and paid for the bedding I planned to die in. Drove home in the half-light.

The boxes were back in the living room. The pale man nowhere to be seen. I found a pair of scissors and cut the tape.

ELÍN, PAPERS

At first, I'd written in cheap spiral notebooks. When I was sixteen years old, my grandma gave me a beautiful book with angels on it. I wrote everything with a fountain pen. The ink, light blue. Blots like fat tears in the margins. The script cramped yet slapdash.

Grandma made a wig you can't put on your head.

(. . .)

I came home at midnight and there was a candle burning right on top of the table.

(. . .)

She said she knew exactly what I was planning.

(. . .)

I am afraid.

(. . .)

She doesn't know if it's day or night.

(. . .)

My face is a mold full of hardening concrete.

(. . .)

No one visits or calls.

(. . .)

I'm afraid to leave her alone when I go to school.

I paged through the book. Read sentences here and there. Somehow, I'd always imagined that I'd go like Grandma. That my mind would empty itself until its commands ceased being carried out by my body. The prospect had terrified me ever since I said goodbye to her. The thought terrified me so much that I never finished it. It traveled along with me unthought, shaped me, found a channel through me. The fear of losing my mind.

I knew exactly what became of women like me. We walked through the streets with plastic bags tied over our wool-stockinged feet, muttering to ourselves in a never-ending conversation and we lay down in doorways, parking garages, on top of grates, resting our weary bones at the library until we were thrown out.

WE.

I would be thrown out because I never bathed, because I didn't know how water worked anymore. Because it was inexplicably annoying when wet drops irritated my skin and completely pointless.

Is there nothing that can be done to help the woman? people would whisper to one another. That's what she wants, said others, puzzled, and no one helped the woman. No one knew her well enough before she got sick to know that she didn't want to sleep on a grate.

When I came home today, Grandma was scared. She said she'd seen people in the living room, tiny people dressed in colorful clothes. She said they lived in the corner behind the sofa, and that I should just see if I didn't see them myself. They move so fast, she said, skitter and jingle like silver on crystal. I asked her if it wasn't just mice, but she said they were dressed in purple velvet and had golden hair and drank from a tiny china service with their little fingers crooked in the air. I saw nothing behind the sofa but dust and dirt.

(. . .)

She looked out the window and said that the lambs had arrived. They were lying out there with the little children, and there was a halo around them.

A divine halo.

When she was sixteen years old, Ellen stopped taking part in the annual poetry competition that was named after her father. She also stopped writing poetry and focused her attention on a newfound desire to do well in school. She took a job in the evenings and on weekends selling subscriptions to a science magazine over the phone, bought herself a new pair of shoes and a backpack for her schoolbooks, and got a computer that she paid for in installments with a dedicated student loan.

She attended her lectures cool and blank faced but trembling under it all for fear of screwing up, misunderstanding something, making errors in her arithmetic, saying something wrong, embarrassing herself. She said as little as possible and avoided the few people she knew from grade school. She wanted to have her own life, unadulterated by all the weirdness that had enveloped her for as long as she could remember.

In her literature course, the class read her dad's first novel. A story he wrote when he was right around twenty and which had been a huge success. It was about an old man who was caring for his ancient father. This narrative was interwoven with that of a mother and daughter who rented the attic apartment in their house and grappled with extreme poverty. The daughter's name was Ellen, and she was the bright spot in the story—pretty, clever, good, and working her fingers to the bone to save herself and her mother from the clutches of poverty.

Just before the end of the book, there was a long chapter that told of Ellen taking a job as a migrant worker during the haymaking season and getting paid per bag of hay. Her mother had terrible joint pain, and they didn't have enough for medicine to treat it, which is why she hit upon this scheme.

Then it started to rain. Most people stopped working, but Ellen cut and cut, then was cut down in her prime; several weeks later, she wasted away from pneumonia and died. Downstairs, the story continued uneventfully. The two old men, father and son, drank down all sorts of infusions and tinctures and lived out their lives in warmth, reminiscing on the old days.

The students analyzed the text, and Ellen tried to look at what her father had written without thinking about herself. What he wrote was just words, just words that had been arranged on paper, striving for meaning. The teacher wasn't drowning in reverence, just skated over this and that so they'd get to reading the next book on the list. Was clearly bored of teaching *My Father* by Álfur Finnsson.

One Saturday night, she went to a party with her classmates and talked to a girl she'd noticed in the hallway at school. The girl was often alone, like Ellen, and dressed in clothes that were unfashionable—in a deliberate way. Her hair was scruffy, bangs hanging over her eyes, and she wore a leather string around her neck that seemed uncomfortably tight.

She said her name was Birta and offered Ellen a beer. Birta was from a different town and didn't know anyone. It took her almost an hour to get to school. Ellen asked why she hadn't gone to a school in her own neighborhood, and then Birta said she'd been bullied so much there that she'd have actually preferred to go to school even farther away.

She fell silent. Ellen was uncomfortable.

Ooops, said Birta, adding bitterly that this was exactly why she'd gotten bullied.

What do you mean? asked Ellen, and Birta said she'd promised her mom that she wouldn't tell anyone at her new school about the bullying.

Because now you'll stop talking to me and tell your friends that I'm a victim, and they'll pick up my scent and the problem will just continue.

Victim?

Yeah, Mom's always saying that people are either victims or victimizers . . .

I get it, said Ellen, but fortunately for you, I don't have any friends.

Were you also bullied?

No, and I don't understand why. It's incredible, actually, said Ellen. I'm sure it's all thanks to Rakel, the girl in my class who was bullied.

Poor Rakel.

Cheers to Rakel.

To Rakel.

On Monday, they met up during their break and went to the mall. Birta taught Ellen how to shoplift beauty products, and Ellen made up a game in which they hid on the uppermost floor and spit on the heads of people on the ground floor. They didn't hit anyone for the most part, although one time, they did succeed, and then they laughed so hard that Birta almost peed her pants, and then they felt horribly guilty and tried to justify themselves by making up awful stories about the man they'd spat on.

Then the security guard showed up, but they managed to get away from him on foot. As they ran, something came loose. Ellen ran and laughed and something came loose from its moorings, and then she was bawling. So much that she couldn't catch her breath, so much that her limbs stiffened and her fingers clenched. Birta put her arms around her, held her tight, and was quiet until Ellen calmed down again.

Should I go home with you? she asked gently, but Ellen couldn't get a word out.

Do you want to come home with me? she asked then hesitantly. My dad's going to grill lamb chops and it's Friday, so no school tomorrow, and you can just stay over at our place.

Resourceful and clear headed. A little maternal. Ellen nodded. They waited for the bus in the twilight. Birta suggested that Ellen call her mother, but Ellen couldn't speak. She tried to, but then started to sob all over again.

Birta's house looked like it had been dug out of the lava, with green-and-white wood siding like a hobbit dwelling, Ellen thought. Birta's parents were on the older side, and she was an only child.

Her dad was wearing welding gloves, shivering outside in the chilly evening and turning the lamb chops. Her mom sat at the kitchen table, which was stacked high with books and papers. She had a pair of reading glasses on her nose and another pair on her forehead. Her hair was bushy and standing on end, grizzled and yellow.

When she heard their footsteps, she switched glasses, peered at Ellen, and then smiled like a shark. Birta rolled her eyes and introduced them.

Birta's bedroom was essentially the room of a child. A bedroom that had last been painted back before she was confirmed, before she started having opinions about colors. On the walls, there were pictures of cats that had been clipped from the tops of chocolate boxes as well as a number of cut-out and framed pictures of Birta and her parents from over the years. A big poster with a picture of David Bowie. His eyes were closed and there was a pastel lightning bolt across his face.

On the floor, there were piles of clothes and scraps of food and half-full soda bottles and blobs of gum and dust that jumped up on your socks when you moved. Birta switched on a lamp, turned off the ceiling light. The bed was unmade. A dirt-smudged white shade was pulled down over the window.

I hate everything that's mundane, said Birta and Ellen asked why.

I mean, just things and picking up and washing your hands . . .

You don't wash your hands?

Yeah, I mean, I definitely do. I wash my hands, but just because you're always supposed to, every single time you go to the bathroom. It's all the time. And just, going to the bathroom. But still, mostly picking up. And buying things and eating and throwing out the wrappers and waiting for the bus.

Prosaic, said Ellen.

We should stop, she said.
What do you mean?
Just stop doing everything we don't want to do.
Just piss our pants.
Just in our sleep.
And never bathe.
And poop.
Right where you stand.
And then bathe.
No, no, just shake yourself off.
Just remember to shake yourself off.
But eat.
No way.
Go to school.
If you feel like it.
Worry about the future.
What future.
Learn.
Learn what.
Clip your fingernails.
Tear them off.
Bite your fingernails.
Break them off.
Brush your hair.
Pull it out.
Mat your hair.
Hate your hair.
Hide your face.
Hurt your flesh.
Cut the stuff.
Tear it apart.
Slip from the self.

Into the next guy.
Trust no one.
Need nothing.
Want nothing.
Waste nothing.
Lack everything.
Whatever.

Their bedroom walls and their doors dissolved, and the walls converged, their bedrooms opened one into the other but closed at the same time. Became the same bedroom, increased by half, but decreased by a world.

Ellen had never seen herself in another person before. Not except her mother, but now she didn't want to see herself in her mother anymore. She neither wanted to see herself in her mother nor her mother in herself, but her mother was everywhere and nowhere, all-encompassing, yellow and flowing.

Still, most often Birta wanted to stay at Ellen's over the weekend. The thing was, Ellen's mom didn't even notice when they went out at night and didn't come back before morning.

By the start of the spring semester, Ellen had given up all intentions of doing well in school. She didn't even show up for her exams, while Birta did and achieved mixed results without having studied much. Her parents rode her harder, tried to tempt her with family trips to majestic mountains, pets, and really just anything and everything that occurred to them to prolong her childhood.

Ellen, meanwhile, drank and smoked in front of her mother, who had no idea about whether her daughter was working or in school or what. Summer arrived with all its too-bright impetuousness, and Ellen and Birta drifted around town and between parties. Sometimes, something upsetting would happen that neither of them could remember exactly, and they helped each other forget. Scenes in back gardens, in the bedrooms of anonymous children, in the homes of grown adults who laughed at them. They were square pegs in round holes, hard-boiled children. Like dogs wearing sunglasses or infants in dinner jackets. They often slept in their clothes, in each other's arms. Just anywhere. Outside. Wherever they lay their heads. They smoked butts found in ashtrays, got drunk on sips of other people's wine.

That fall, Birta moved to London. Her mother had gotten a job there, and her dad planned to write a book about bricklaying or the utilization of old chimneys or the volume of sewers.

Birta broke the news to her at the last possible moment. She'd known since they met. Had known it was a possibility. Then that it was probable, then definite. They were on their way to the corner store, hung over and craving orange soda. It was starting to get cold, August drawing to an end, and all of a sudden Birta told her.

We're moving to London in two weeks.

Two weeks?

Yeah . . .

How long will you be there?

We're moving there . . . just for a year, or for forever. Mom wants me to go to some crazy boarding school, they have uniforms . . .

But what am I supposed to do?

You can come visit.

I don't even have enough for the bus.

That'll change.

Liar, whispered Ellen, an ugly look on her face.

Birta stopped, looked at her friend wide-eyed. Ellen walked away, went home, and crawled into bed.

That's life, Ellen, honey, said her mom. People come, people go . . .
some without changing anything and others so much so that afterward,
there's nothing but ruin. She sat on the edge of Ellen's bed, her daughter
just staring up at the ripped paper globe that hung around the light and
trying to ignore her mother's words.

Would you like me to tell you about your dad? she asked, and Ellen
turned toward the wall, closed her eyes, and hoped her mom would be
quiet. When Lilja talked about Álfur, Ellen sometimes felt like she was
talking about a piece of Ellen herself, dead and capacious.

Ellen saw this piece in front of her, like a shadow extending from
her own body, and her mom didn't realize that when she went on and
on like this, the shadow got darker and deeper and the void became a
shining black thing, cold and dangerous.

The first time I met your dad, I was three years older than you are now.
He was more than twice my age. He sat so far back in the bar that I
didn't see him, but I felt him and knew he was there, and so when
he came over, I didn't have to look at him to know he was the most
beautiful thing I'd ever seen because he was the most beautiful, Ellen,

the most beautiful thing that has ever existed, and I knew it without needing to see him.

No one has experienced a love like that, no one will experience a love like that again. I didn't see him, never saw him, didn't need to look at him, simply felt that this was my man, my center, the mantle of my life. A person doesn't make decisions like that with their brain, but with their whole body, and it happened instinctively, such that the lines of focus swam before me, my vision weakened, my sense of smell was heightened, my sense of touch changed.

Touching someone who you've decided is your mantle is not like touching. It goes deeper. Much deeper than people usually go. I'm not talking about gratification, but rather, a fact. To be alive. To be a body.

Your consciousness reaches into all the workings of your body. Words are too weak. To have a mantle, a kernel, to orbit. Nothing is stronger. Indescribable. Your dad, Ellen, your dad had a genuine gravitational pull. When he employed it, no one could get away. Nothing he said was predictable or simple.

His wife threw him out, and my dad threw me out. We were just kids, you understand?

But you weren't kids, mumbled Ellen. He was fifty-five and you were twenty.

Her mom was quiet for a moment but then continued as if there'd been no interruption. We were kids, and the world was grown up, and then I got pregnant with you, and his wife was always trying to ruin everything. She hurt him so badly. You should know how she spoke to him. The things she said to him were so ugly that I tried to talk to her, but she just screamed and used the children. They were teenagers then, and she used them against him.

You can't imagine, Ellen, how cruel people can be. She came to our place with the children to show them how much of a loser their dad was, and they cried, and their dad cried, and she always called me "that child." Never looked at me. Never spoke to me. Not a word. Never. She hated me even more than him, just for existing.

We just wanted to feel things and be alive and in the moment and together and paint and let the words flow and he wanted to drink less and my stomach got bigger and she screamed and he got more and more depressed and drank and then he was going to go back to her and I told him I would die. That's what I thought, that we would die, and he left but he came right back, all scratched up. His sweet skin all scratched, and it was then that I saw him for the first time.

When he came back all scratched up. Came back to us.

That's when I looked at him for the first time. All at once, I saw how life had toyed with him. You see everything on people—experience collects on them, everything is there to see, and yet, few give themselves the time to read it. Your dad could read it, and he described it for the rest of us, that was his work, but I could also read him when I saw him for the first time. He appeared to me in myriad layers and folds. So complex but at the same time, so transparent.

A fifty-nine-year-old man. Uncared for in infancy. Cheated of guidance. Humiliated. Isolated. Uncared for. Worshipped. Beloved. Cheated of discipline. Of understanding. An explanation. A caress. A living soul that springs from apathy. A miracle. Feels pleasure. Stays for a time, latches on, gets stuck. Goes away. Gets stuck. Goes away. Grows arrogant. Postures. Trusts no one. Sees no one. Not really. Feels nothing. Not really. Fades. Gets stuck. A soul that's born of apathy and dies of it again. A miracle. Goes away. Gets stuck in its pose. Stuck for years on end. All crooked. Grays. The flow subsides. Stiffens. Wails. Tries to inch away. Chafes itself free. Paws itself a tunnel. Finally slicks itself down with pleasure. Dries up. Copulates in the slick.

A fifty-nine-year-old man. Rubbish around a hole. Rubbish around a bottomless, black, fucking hole. Every word he wrote begged for love, for guidance and discipline and understanding and explanation, but they were just words read by idiots and didn't matter, don't matter, idiots don't matter nor the words that idiots read.

I looked at your dad and I saw him.

Saw your dad and saw that he thought he was attaining immortality. That he thought others would die, but he would live forever through the little words he wrote for the little blockheads that read them. That's why his face was so gray, why he was so drawn and all his muscles so inflamed and stiff, and that was why he drank so much, in the hope of stimulating the flow, but he was stuck. Stuck and petrified by the fear of death.

And then, of course, he died, simply because fear is never without cause, and I nearly died with him but fortunately, I had you

and you saved me.

Ellen stopped going to school but kept her shifts at the call center. She'd gotten good at making people believe they needed science magazines. She'd sit and recite rehearsed speeches on the phone and then catch the bus home to take care of Lilja.

Which was a little like filling the role of atmosphere. The things that Lilja said and did were seldom intended for anyone else. Words that rang out and then were no more. Like her thoughts. Food was either on the table in front of her and she ate—or not, and she went hungry. The only thing she took care of herself were cigarettes, which she bought from a nearby corner store. Five cartons at the start of every month.

The suffocating feeling and the desire for security converged as one and, as what remained of that winter passed, Ellen felt worse and worse. She'd hear from Birta in London every once in a while, but answered late, and badly. Sometimes, she'd go out and meet up with acquaintances, not say anything, and drink.

The wires have been severed, she thought once, and then one night at the end of November, when she lay numb in her bed and couldn't even be bothered to open her computer or phone, she dozed and dreamed.

An empty, darkened stage and an auditorium full of people. There was a root lying in the middle of the stage. It moved and sprouted downward into the black floor and then grew like a beanstalk up into the air. The plant grew quickly, thin shoots that branched out again and again until it stretched across the whole stage and up in the air, under and through the bleachers and in through the audience, wrenching the viewers up into the air and throwing them into a pile in the middle of the stage.

She snapped awake and reached for her computer. The play flowed from her so steadily that she felt like someone had taken up residence inside her and was using her fingers on the keyboard.

The change wasn't immediate, not before page twenty, and then all of a sudden, she noticed something in her surroundings, an unusually sharp stillness, or the northern lights over the bay. The attentiveness was new, cut through her apathy, and she kept writing, wrote until there was space. About the size of a fist or a heart, and she breathed differently. The sound was gone, the wheezy, choking sound. There was a slackening at her throat.

Her thoughts fired off better in her mind, achieved a beginning and an end. She took out books from the library and read. She wrote another play and then finally the third, which she was the most satisfied with. It was called *Feathers and Sinews*, eighty pages about a young man and his father, uncle, and grandfather.

The night she finished the play, the shadow disappeared. Her mom was sitting in the kitchen and when Ellen came in to get something from the fridge, she looked at her daughter and said:

Something's different about you.

Ellen was startled. She wasn't used to having Lilja pay attention to her.

I finished a play, said Ellen and smiled.

May I hear it? asked Lilja, and Ellen said she was self-conscious about reading it out loud.

We'll read it together, said Lilja, and in the end Ellen relented. They sat side by side in the living room and took turns reading. Lilja's eyes brimmed with tears, and she interrupted the reading over and over with her cries of admiration.

When they finished reading, she said that Ellen should send the play to the theater. You've got nothing to lose by doing it, she said. Two months later, Ellen sent *Feathers and Sinews* to the theater's artistic director. She wasn't expecting any kind of response, but she got a return message to the effect that the play was going to be read by the artistic committee that made the decisions about what plays were staged by the theater. The artistic director also asked whether she was right in assuming that Ellen was the daughter of the author Álfur Finnsson and whether she wasn't indeed still under the age of twenty?

Ellen replied and said she was right on both counts. She only had to wait a week before the artistic director called and invited her to a meeting. Everyone on the committee agreed that the play was good, and they most definitely wanted the theater to buy it from Ellen and debut it in the coming season.

Lilja started talking about them in the plural. They were going to premiere their play at the theater. Their play would be so popular. On some occasions, her first-person plural shifted to a first-person singular.

Lilja was going to premiere her play at the theater; her play would be a huge success. Ellen would feel a bit dizzy but let it roll off her back like she was used to doing, and they were going to premiere and Lilja was so happy that Ellen didn't have the heart to correct her.

The night before the first read-through, Ellen came to the realization that her mom thought they were going to attend it together.

Mama, I think it would be better if I went by myself, Ellen screwed up her courage to say.

I'll be with you in spirit, her mother replied stridently, after a little consideration, and then continued rummaging through her closet. The next morning, when Ellen came out in a rush, her mom was sitting in the hallway, ready to go.

Mom, I can't take you with me to the reading, said Ellen as gently as she could, but this time, it was though Lilja hadn't even heard her. She got to her feet, quivering with childlike excitement, and Ellen lost her patience.

Mom, you are not coming with me, she said with determination. This is a read-through of my play, not yours! She hurried into the bathroom where she brushed her teeth with a shaky hand, splashed water on her face, realized that she was going to be late, ran back into her bedroom, and pulled on the first clothes she saw.

Dirty gym socks and a pilled T-shirt with an advertisement for a pharmaceutical company on the front, track pants with snaps down the sides, and a patterned sweater with a gray cotton hood. She shoved her feet into a pair of patent-leather shoes in the vestibule, looked at her mother and said brusquely:

Goodbye!

At the start of every month, Lilja received a disability payment of 230,000 krónur, about $2,000. Up until Ellen turned eighteen, she got an additional $600 or so in child support and, finally, a family allowance of up to $300.

This is to say that on Ellen's eighteenth birthday, Lilja lost almost a third of the money she'd been living on. Ellen promised to pitch in for her upkeep, but the wages she received were just so low. They had little choice but to deny themselves anything that could even possibly be called surplus to necessity, except, of course, cigarettes. Cigarettes were like electricity. And a few cartons of wine. Like water. And then, of course, a few bottles of liquor—to help Lilja sleep.

When Ellen signed her contract with the theater and the first payment—half a million krónur, around $4,500—was deposited into her account, she and her mom went out to eat. They ate lobster and steak and drank red wine and ordered a second bottle and then a third and got some kind of soufflé for dessert, and Lilja talked of regret, of how poor people turned themselves into vending machines that exchange regrets for krónur, and Ellen said no, no, and then they talked about Lilja's debts while they drank coffee and cognac.

Ellen was a little tipsy, and before she knew it, she'd offered to pay off the debts with her payment, and Lilja became so overjoyously grateful that Ellen said she'd also pay off the apartment in a few months. She had, after all, always lived there for free—her whole childhood and as a teenager, too. Then maybe Lilja could do something for herself, like get a massage or even go to a sanatorium in the French Alps. Or just to the dentist.

Thus did they let themselves dream about all the things they could do with Ellen's payment. Lilja had long wanted to try acupuncture, and they'd never gone abroad together. Actually, Ellen had never been abroad at all, and Lilja only twice when she was little, and then only to Denmark both times.

Ellen wanted to go to London, but Lilja said they should go instead to the Kerala region in India and sail down the Pamba River while people chanted back and forth across the banks.

Just imagine, she said with her eyes closed. The voices in the twilight and the black jungle and the tranquility.

For the briefest moment, it crossed Ellen's mind that she should buy a single one-way plane ticket to India for Lilja, but the shame that flared up in the wake of that thought made her forget it in the very same moment. Lilja opened her eyes, smiled, and said that now everything was going to be okay for them. Ellen would be a rich and famous author and could look after them both and maybe buy a Cadillac for Lilja—pink like Elvis got for his mom.

Ellen cringed and felt a little claustrophobic but shook it off. After she paid the dinner bill, Ellen no longer had $4,500, but $4,000.

The play was total garbage. Ellen heard it herself and knew in the same moment that the only reason the theater intended to stage it was that she, Ellen, was Ellen. Her father's daughter. And because the play was about fathers. The working title was *Feathers and Sinews*, which she'd thought would be a fun play on *Fathers and Sons* by Turgenev. The theater would sell masses of tickets. Everyone would want to know what Ellen had to say about her father. They'd want to see her father resurrected.

All the things that people could sense that the widow left publicly unsaid. All the things that Ellen's mother whispered to the walls in their home, mumbled into her cigarettes and into Ellen's still-impressionable head.

Ellen was so preoccupied with these thoughts that she didn't even notice that the director was belittling her. There was so much noise from her own personal demolition that she didn't hear the words *pivot* and *turning point*.

Similarly, she didn't feel the cold until she was the better part of the way home. She'd walked as though in a trance but came to all at once and saw the car of the old lady from the props department. Elín's car.

My car. The squarish, rusty SUV that I'd offered her a ride in the day before. Why was I following her? Did I think Ellen wouldn't notice? Was I planning to offer her a ride again?

No. I slowed down. Ellen acted as though she didn't notice anything. She thought I seemed perfectly harmless. Off-putting at the very worst, but that was merely a side effect of loneliness. She just thought it was strange that the prop lady had started following her and considered why that might be.

Maybe it had to do with her father, like most other things in Ellen's life. Something that happened back before she was even born. Maybe the props lady had a crush on her, it suddenly occurred to Ellen, and she found that a little funny.

They'd make a great couple. Like a Before and After shot.

The cold feeling intensified.

Why do I do that? thought Ellen.

Over and over.

Why are my feet so cold?

Lilja sat still in the kitchen when Ellen came in, whimpering from the cold. You could hear a pin drop, and when she looked in through the yellow cloud of smoke, she saw her mother at the end of the table, her head lying in front of her on the table and her hair draping—mussed, yellow, and long—all over her like a quilt.

Mama? she asked gently. Mama, are you okay?

She didn't hear anything for a moment, but then Lilja raised her head.

Were you napping, Mama?

Yes, just resting my eyes for a moment, answered Lilja, lighting a cigarette and looking out the window.

Is there someone following you? she asked and pointed. Ellen walked over and looked out onto the parking lot by the apartment building, saw the prop lady's SUV and stormed back out, down the stairs and out into the lot. Barged over and banged on the hood.

There I sat, intent on my phone; I jumped. Then I got out and looked at Ellen, stock-still, and didn't say a word.

Stop following me! she yelled. The last thing I need is some old lesbo obsessing over me!

When she saw my expression, she immediately regretted having said what she said. She always rejected people at least three times before opening herself up to them, just like me, and just like me, she regretted it every time.

She went back in to her mother and meant to go straight to her room, but then Lilja was standing there, pale as death, asking if that had been Elín Jónsdóttir in the car.

I don't know, said Ellen. She makes props and yes, her name is maybe Elín, something with an E . . .

She's the one who found your father, said Lilja, grabbing her face in horror, as if Elín Jónsdóttir had just found her father in that very moment.

In Romania, there are living stones that grow and multiply. Every breath takes three days and they move less than an inch a month, but they breathe. They move.

They're called *trovants*, or "sandstone concretions," and when you cut them in half, they have growth rings, like trees. I first read about them in an article in a science magazine that Ellen sold me a subscription to over the phone. I cut out a picture of them and hung it on the wall and have often looked at them on the internet, but I've never gone to see them in Romania. Like misshapen hippos partially disguised by water, in another time, from another realm, among us.

This happens under an entirely unique set of biological prerequisites. The right amount of calcium in the soil, a precise amount of humidity in the air, etc. A series of optimizations and details. A monkey eats a nut, shits in the right soil, up grows a particular flower, which is eaten by a certain bird, which in turn flies over a specific kind of sand, shits, and up grows a bush, and the bush burns to withered stalks, which produce seeds, and an ape shows up, and so on and so forth. Repetitive, gradual, and dull.

Aloneness is the most contemptuous illusion, I thought when I read about the trovants. This perception that makes it so the threads between me and those stones, between me and all those people who trudge facelessly through my life—into it and out of it again—don't seem to exist. How I pretend that my thoughts are mine alone, as if no one has thought them before, as if no one is thinking them right now. And now and now and now.

The exact same thoughts.

Álfur Finnsson polished off a pint of landi, stuck another bottle in his pocket, went out over Lilja's protestations. Where did he plan on going that drunk, why? she cried, and he grunted and staggered and fell on the landing when he tried to pull on his shoes, having long since become too inarticulate for anyone to be able to make out a word he was saying.

Ellen was asleep in her crib. They'd been sitting and talking and smoking and had exhausted all happiness. Instead of reflecting one another back to each other and creating their own world, they'd gotten annoyed and hurt, and Laufey, Álfur's wife, was there with them, an invisible presence in the living room, along with all the teenagers' bawling and Álfur's guilt.

Álfur said he was back for good, that he would never leave her again, but Lilja said she didn't believe that for a second, and Álfur got mad, and Lilja got hurt, and that's how they ended up in the same rut night after night, usually until Álfur became incoherent and then fell asleep.

He hadn't written anything for months and blamed it on them, Lilja and Laufey, those women who couldn't get enough of him.

There's too little of me for the two of you, he blathered and became incoherent, but instead of going to sleep, he wanted to go out and drink some more.

I've got to get out of here, he said, but Lilja didn't catch it. He tripped on the landing. She got into bed. It was 2:00 a.m. She was exhausted. He'll have gone back to Laufey, she thought, and Ellen stirred. Lilja gave in to temptation and picked her up, looked at the little sleep-drunk face and hugged her to herself.

Mama, mumbled Ellen. It was the only word she said, in spite of the fact that she was two years old. She took a lock of Lilja's hair in her little hand and pulled, and when Lilja squeaked, she laughed such that the little pearls in her mouth shone. They fell asleep in Lilja and Álfur's bed and then, two hours later, Lilja woke up, her eyes wide with the certainty that something terrible had happened. At first, she ran outside alone, but quickly remembered Ellen and turned around, gathered the sleeping child in her arms, ran down the steps, and out into the street.

It was probably about 4:00 a.m. I'd been out with Fjóla, who was far too drunk. She was newly divorced and had moved back to Iceland. I sometimes ended up in this role and had babysat her all night, fended off men who had a mind to take advantage of her drunkenness and pulled her off whatever random stranger she'd thrown herself at, got reproaches for my trouble—got hit with her handbag, even—brought her back home, and left her, still wearing all her clothes, on top of her bedcovers, muttering something about her divorce. Then I started walking home.

Álfur was lying about a hundred yards from the place where a few days earlier we'd met and talked about nothing in particular. He was in such a strange position that I saw right away that he was dead. I bent over him, laid my palm on his forehead. His eyes were open and I closed them. Wearing a green-gray coat with black leather gloves, his face white as chalk.

In his pockets he had a blue pack of Gauloises cigarettes with two cigarettes in it, one of them broken right at the filter, a brown leather wallet with a credit card and two crumpled thousand-krónur bills, a key to his wife's house, and another to his girlfriend's.

If you were to look at a map of the location where I came upon him that morning, you'd see that it was precisely the same distance to his wife's home and to his girlfriend's, and that he died, therefore, smack dab in the middle.

My own theory is that he did this unconsciously on purpose, just like people do in fiction. Just a few days before, I ran into him not far from that spot, we stopped for a moment and chatted and smoked and based on what I'd read and seen of Álfur, it was exactly the kind of thing he would do—dramatize and stage his own life. There was often a character in his novels who was entirely in the thrall of his emotions, and the reader followed along with his way of thinking until they could put themselves in the character's shoes and understand the most peculiar behavior.

Gulping down a whole pint of landi smack dab in between the women he loved had, more to the point, an aesthetic quality that reminded me of one of his stories. Matte-white plastic with a red cap, a river of vomit, an empty bottle, and a corpse. Just like the melodramatic climax in a story by Álfur Finnsson.

I touched his face, felt that rigor mortis had already started to set in. His coat was open and I went to button it, completely illogically, but then I came upon the pack of cigarettes in his inside pocket and took out one of the two—the unbroken one—and lit it.

Bless you, dust, I whispered and felt his presence. Felt how he swirled, drunken and free, and blended with the smoke from the cigarette. When I closed his eyes, I saw how he shifted—earth and man and earth and man and earth and man—in a flash, in my mind's eye.

This scene never ended. It played out before me on an eternal loop. Trauma is, of course, nothing but an enchantment:

I saw Lilja. She came walking around the corner with a little girl in her arms. In a shearling-lined suede coat and the little girl not but two years old at the most, wrapped in a mottled blanket and hanging on to her mother with red splotches on her cheeks and bareheaded in the cold. I walked determinedly toward them and took Lilja by the shoulder.

I'm searching, she said and looked over my shoulder, saw Álfur, called out.

Come with me, I said, we have to call an ambulance.

Is he asleep? she asked, and I shook my head. Reminded her of the girl by saying hello to her.

Aren't you a pretty little girl? I said, and then Lilja handed her to me and walked over to Álfur. She was cold, and I stuck her under my coat and her mother's howls sliced through the stillness of the night, rousing the residents of the neighborhood.

Someone called an ambulance. The paramedics and police officers arrived quickly, silent and serious. The body was placed on a stretcher. Lilja was inconsolable. I suggested that I should take the child somewhere indoors, but they didn't let me. An old woman appeared and argued with the officers until we were allowed to go to her house. We sat in her living room.

Ellen didn't say a word, but her eyes were like saucers and she was watching everything happening around her. I thought about how this would affect her, whether and what she understood. The blue police lights blinked through the window. Her mother's cries filtered into the living room, to the old woman who came in with tea biscuits and a glass of milk.

The walls were covered with photographs of children—she was obviously an old hand. It crossed my mind to pass the girl over to her, but then the child tightened her grip on me. Her hair was thin and blonde, like silk, and it tickled my nose. Her heart rate was unusually rapid, and I realized she was silent because she was afraid.

A young police officer came in. He said that the mother was looking for her child. The old woman said there was no sense in giving her the child in the state she was in. The police officer nodded, then frowned.

Is there no one who can come? Some relative?

She says there's no one.

Then you'll have to ask again, said the granny, because she's not getting the child in her state. Tell her the moppet is with a woman who's been a grandmother eight times over and a great-grandmother four times over, and we're going to have a glass of milk and biscuits, and then maybe the child will have a snooze in the hammock.

The police officer went out again, and we sat in the blinking lights. Little Ellen wanted nothing to do with the milk and biscuits. She just clutched on to my coat, and I tried to recall a lullaby, but didn't remember anything of the sort, so I just hummed the snatch of some song quietly next to her ear.

Not long after, her mother's cries fell silent, or at least got farther away, and the cars drove off. The police officer came in again and told us that the child's grandmother was on the way, but that it would take her at least an hour to get to us.

He took a seat in the living room with us, and we talked about this and that. The old woman steered the conversation, dead set on lightening the mood. Slowly but surely, Ellen's little heart slowed down, and I felt her pulling air all the way down into her body.

Lilja had masses of acquaintances and friends with whom she had different degrees of contact, but who were always there on the sidelines, rambling into her and Ellen's life and then out of it again. Lilja had lovers who introduced her and Ellen to their parents, or even to their children. Girlfriends who parted company with their men and sought out companionship until they disappeared again into their next relationship.

For a time, Lilja's drawings were somewhat in fashion. She exhibited them in museums and galleries, and people came to their apartment and bought pictures. Lilja taught the occasional course at the arts college.

Ellen's grandma and grandpa, Lilja's parents, lived out in the countryside and didn't have much to do with them. They had other children who were doing quite well for themselves and whom they didn't have to worry about, unlike Lilja and all her misfortune, the heartache she never seemed able to get over. People got mixed up in all sorts of things and got over them, but their Lilja was different.

Sometimes, she went through periods where she cut back on her drinking, went to a psychologist, received diagnoses that fit just about perfectly—or well enough, at least—for a time. She'd feel like she understood something, like she was seeing her life from outside of herself. Her unhealthy patterns and how she got close to people, so close, in fact, that the big picture was lost, and the only thing she could see was herself, weeping, in their pupils. All of the diagnoses were right; all of them were wrong.

Hidden in Lilja's head were disappointments, buried deep in her hippocampus, in her amygdala, in her thalamus, in her limbic cortex, like land mines, and they changed her perception of the world.

At first glance, her life might seem entirely erratic and absent of any kind of routine, but Ellen knew that every day had its rising action, pivots, and climax. Then a lung would appear, fill with air, ever more air, and then breathe out, ever more air, slow and steady, until night had fallen. The days started and ended, and Lilja's illness was within bounds and everything that was within those bounds was manageable.

Not being able to go to the bank was bad but could generally be worked around by Ellen accessing her online bank account for her, or calling the customer service center.

That was within bounds.

Reading about the medicinal benefits of turmeric and opening a spice jar, seeing the shade of yellow—this almost phosphorescent color that stuck to everything—and rubbing it everywhere. On herself and the kitchen table and the curtains and in her hair, on her cigarettes and the windowpanes.

Yellow.

Blurring together with her daughter was perfectly ordinary and had happened since Ellen was born. Ordinary. Commonplace. They were such great friends.

Way out of bounds.

After she saw me through the window, Lilja's routine started to fall apart. Erratic pivots disrupted the lung's expansion and Lilja deteriorated.

Ellen decided they shouldn't stage the play. She didn't know how that sort of thing worked and so just sent the director an email and said she was calling it off. She didn't understand how her decision might affect other people's lives, and the director got angry.

She'd sold her play to the theater, had received two of the three payments, and people were on the payroll. The set designer had constructed boxes, and the people in the wig department had gotten started. Every single hair in every single wig was being threaded by hand by a person being paid by the hour. Did she not understand anything? Was she not aware of all the rehearsals in which the actors repeated her words onstage, all the nuance that was being put into her words? All the training that was needed to instill a specific nuance at a specific point, all the emotions and all the education?

Did she not understand anything?

My mom is ill, she tried to explain.

Actors go on with dead babies in their wombs if there's a show, said Hreiðar, and hung up.

I didn't respond to her apology text, and although it crossed her mind to get in touch with me, she didn't dare. Then on the opening night of her play, she was sitting in the waiting room of the psychiatric ward with her mom.

Her doctor had advised them to go there, and Ellen suspected it was because he'd hoped that Ellen would have a few nights off, more than anything. However, her mom never said anything about harming herself or anyone else, and as such, they were usually sent back home.

The RN on duty asked what medication she was taking, whether she was getting any sleep or eating at all, and Ellen said that neither of them was getting any sleep or eating and that Lilja was in desperate need of help.

She's totally cracking up, will you please help her, for god's sake, said Ellen, and Lilja looked at her skeptically from under the hood of her sweater.

Are you sure that you don't need help? she whispered, and Ellen closed her eyes. She collapsed into her chair and sat there, motionless. Her face hardened like a cast, her skull filled with concrete that then hardened. When she opened her eyes again, the RN had gone to consult with a doctor, which Ellen knew was a good sign.

Her mom looked at her and then started shaking from pent-up laughter. She was so absurdly childlike and pretty. Ellen sometimes felt like a beached whale next to her. A misshapen mass, dead of natural causes. Meat for a whole village.

When Ellen was ten years old, maybe eleven, she and Lilja drove to the Snæfellsnes peninsula together. This was in the summer. Back before the country was filled with tourists and when the glacier was still clearly visible on the horizon. They took a day trip. Set off at the crack of dawn in the dented compact car that Lilja owned.

They were in a good mood, listened to the oldies station and crunched on cinnamon candies on empty stomachs. Lilja would think of a person, and Ellen had to guess who it was.

Is he young?

Yes.

Is he Icelandic?

No.

Is he a musician?

Yes.

Do I listen to him?

Sometimes, although you might not admit it . . .

Is he from Canada?

Yes.

Is it Justin Bieber?

How did you know?

Easy.

They drove into the peninsula, were going to head toward the glacier and eat a picnic lunch in the sun. Then they were going to go to Stykkishólmur, where Lilja wanted to see a performance that some acquaintance of hers was going to put on at the art museum that had opened there.

There was a sign on the side of the road on which someone had written *Hvalreki—Beached Whale*—and an arrow that pointed to the coastline. Lilja parked the car and they got out, walked down to the beach. The sun was shining high and warm in the sky, but there was still enough chill in the air that Ellen zipped up her coat and picked her way across the tussocks with her hands in her pockets.

Golden plover chirruped amid the dry yellow grass. It had turned green in some places, but in others there were still patches of ice thawing. When they'd climbed over the stone wall and come down on the other side, Ellen's tennis shoes were sucked into the pink sand, and she clapped her hand over her nose.

A rotting sperm whale carcass was lying a few hundred yards away. The bones had been strewn all over the place by animals and people alike, and the skin was still intact in some places, turned white and somewhat sludgy. The fresh sea air carried with it the stench of decay.

Look, there's the skull! said Lilja, running over the sand.

It's like an easy chair! she called and took a seat on the skull, waving Ellen over.

The art museum was located on a cliff. The gallery floor was green foam, and the windows stretched across the whole wall. Out beyond them, the ocean glittered, breaking on boulders as seals' heads appeared and disappeared and black-backed gulls flew over in throngs. At the far end of the room stood the performance artist, a man around forty dressed in a tweed suit and a red-brown turtleneck with his back turned to the audience, ten or so people who stood waiting to see what would happen next.

After a short time, the man turned around to the audience. His eyes were closed and he took his hands out of his pockets, lifted one and opened his fist with trembling fingers. Then he lifted the other hand and it was trembling, too. His head shook and then his shoulders started to spasm. He lifted his hands and before long, he was shaking violently all over. He cried out and seemed to be trying to restrain himself, without success.

The shaking just became worse, the shouting. As though he was being attacked. But there was nothing there.

They admitted Lilja for respite care. Ellen stood on the sidewalk in front of the hospital and pictured the last scene before the intermission—the dad tumbling around with the grandfather, the son brawling with the uncle, and the hole that opens beneath them, swallowing the whole stage and then darkness.

At this point in the story, it's perhaps important for me to admit something. From the moment I saw Ellen at the theater and up until the opening night of her play, I spied on her and her mom.

Not constantly, of course, but periodically. I didn't park in the parking lot in the dark and look through their windows with binoculars, but I found everything you could think of online. I read obituaries for their family members and sometimes, I followed them. That happened, yes. It happened that I sat in a cold car in the parking lot and watched the lights flickering in their windows, and yes, I may have used binoculars.

In general, I thought about them and made them into characters, who became dear to me. I breathed life into them, if you can say that, and I felt like I knew them. The better that I felt I knew them, the more absurd the idea of getting close to them in real life became.

After the premiere, I drove in circles around their apartment building and thought about Ellen's play and a book by Álfur Finnsson. *Dust*, it was called, and it might have been the book of his that enjoyed the least popularity. It was a short novel about a middle-aged man who wanders around the city in search of something that would give his life meaning.

Like a prince in a fable, he asks different oracles for advice, but the answers he gets are wrong and lead him even further astray. Then, just before the end of the book, it comes to light that waiting at home for him are a wife and young children, and they are hungry.

Because without him, they don't get fed? I wondered and then I saw her walk by. Her body language was, no doubt about it, that of a person who's at the end of their tether. Poor child, I thought, and for a moment, I considered offering her a ride again.

I didn't.

I made the decision to forget Ellen and her mom and their misfortunes.

As if I didn't have enough of my own.

I went home and walked in circles and opened the boxes and peeked in and closed them again and dealt with project requests and got things done and time passed. Days, weeks, months.

Helen, the girl from upstairs, is always asking me to fix the broken light fixture on the landing. I just say no. I discovered a new kind of tea biscuit that was bad enough that I could keep a package in the cupboard for more than half an hour, but still good enough that I didn't forget about it until after they had expired.

The girl upstairs got a cat without talking to me about it first and I scolded her, but we quickly made peace afterward. She's all right. The cat's a pain in the ass, comes and goes as he likes and doesn't shut up until I've given him something to eat.

Bright orange and furry as anything with impudent eyes that win every staring contest. She calls it Frowny. Or Brownie. Something with an *ow*. Maybe Meowie. Her oldest boy got to name the cat. The youngest is still just tiny and the one in the middle doesn't say much, but I'm not really sure how many of them there are.

Maybe I'm getting mixed up.

Ellen walks along the seaside path parallel to Sæbraut, deep in thought, hopping up onto the seawall every so often. Her light roots have grown a few inches, and her two-tone hair is swept around in the wind. She's wearing a baggy, oversized denim jacket and jeans. The denim is full of holes, and she's got dirty white tennis shoes on her feet. She's wearing headphones. She listens to music and smokes continuously as she hops up on the seawall and then down from it again, and there are no clouds in the sky, just the blue and the winter sun, hanging low.

The night before, she'd met a boy whom she'd been talking to online. He lived in a shed in an industrial neighborhood and smoked opium and knew everything there was to know about addiction and psychological concepts and he wore a track suit and was soft all over like butter and his mom was in jail, but his dad brought him opium, and he kept a big furry spider in a glass box with an infrared light.

They smoked out of a long glass pipe and the light was all red and all the junk in the boy's shed disappeared and his softness became a river and then they lay down, almost too stoned to kiss.

When they woke up in the morning, he put on a pot of coffee and told her, soft-spoken, throatily, as if his mouth was too slack to carve out the words, to be careful because he had borderline personality disorder and was always falling in love with some woman who wasn't there, be it an ex or a next, and Ellen got angry.

Did this polyester-wearing pat of butter think he could reject her? Who exactly did he think he was? That she was? And then she threw on her clothes and stormed out and walked home down Sæbraut.

She'd been home less often of late. Met up with people and learned some new things in the process—how to shake a beer can, stab it with a key, and spray it into her mouth; how to find food that was perfectly fine in dumpsters behind supermarkets and that way, not have to spend money on groceries.

One girl she'd just met, who was a few years older, told her to leave home. She said that Ellen owed her mother nothing and that her mom was an adult and was responsible for all of her own decisions. Ellen kind of wanted to hit the girl, and yet felt that what she was saying was true.

I owe her for giving birth to me, she said, a bit baffled, and the girl said that was crap, total bullshit, and that she should move out as soon as she could. Before it was too late.

But she and her mom had grown apart from one another after Lilja came home from the hospital. Maybe only ever so much, but still enough that Ellen could breathe a bit easier. She had, for instance, definitely noticed that her mom had some little project in the offing, but stopped herself from getting involved.

One morning, Lilja had emptied all the cupboards and closets in the apartment, and clothes and crockery and everything that had been hiding in storage containers and drawers was out on the floor. Ellen assumed it was spring cleaning. Some kind of cleansing.

Things were spread and draped over everything, and her mom was sprawled somewhere poring over something she'd found. Ellen cooked dinner for them but didn't ask her anything about the spring cleaning. Her mom was her usual self, although maybe a little taciturn.

Later, when Ellen was a grown woman and thinking back on this, she saw the shamefaced expression. The escape in her eyes.

And Ellen washed the dishes like she usually did and went into her bedroom and chatted with the boy online and maybe wrote a few paragraphs of a novel she was working on, and then a few days passed and then she was walking along Sæbraut, a bit worked up, and went home and it wasn't before she went into the living room that she figured it out.

If you didn't know better, you might think we're talking about one of those homemade domino experiments where you push a thing and that kicks off everything, and that you can stand and marvel at how the cause becomes the effect becomes the cause becomes the effect for minutes on end, but nothing was cascading, everything was still. No magic happened.

She's gone. Ellen expects to find her body in the bathtub. Expects to find her body in the bedroom. Pictures it so clearly that tears spring to her eyes and she rushes around the apartment, but Lilja is nowhere to be found—she's not in the apartment.

Lilja hasn't driven for years, and yet, the car has disappeared from the parking lot out front. Ellen calls the doctor, calls the police, calls her grandma, calls her new friend, calls the boy who's like butter, calls the phone company, calls the bank. Ellen's account has been emptied. Lilja's account has been closed.

Not long after, she finds out that her mom sold the apartment and the car. That it had all been in the works ever since Ellen sold the play and her mom got the idea to sail down the Pamba River at twilight.

She'll be eaten alive, says her new friend, and then, This is the best thing that could have happened to you, and Ellen slaps her. Her friend's so off her head that she just laughs and hits her back, and Ellen's so off her head that she attacks her friend, who is twice her size and stronger, and who takes her down easily.

Her friend pins her down between her knees, holds her firmly and tells her to try to grow up, to stop her fucking whining, smacks her a few times and then kisses her on the mouth.

Tells her to loosen up

to cry and fight back

to land, sink, dig in her heels.

Like a regular person.

Elín, Books

The Jungle Book, a collection of folktales by Jón Árnason, *Salka Valka* by Halldór Laxness, *Anna Karenina*, a Bible with the names of my mother and grandmother and great-grandmother inscribed on the inside cover. My name was missing. There were three unframed photographs at the bottom of the box. A confirmation photo of me. Apprehensive, my hair set in pin curls, the Bible in my hands, and I'm struck by these hands.

White and smooth and soft and new. They have nothing in common with the hands holding the photo. The other two photographs weren't taken in a photographer's studio, rather ripped from a photo album and put in there along with my books.

As if Grandma had known the album would be taken to the dump, as if she wanted to save these precise photographs. One was taken on a sunny day in some back garden. Grandpa is bare chested, his pants hitched up high, sunglasses on and his head turned toward Grandma.

She's dressed in a bathing suit and smiling. The photo is so overexposed that you can just barely make out her smile, her hair so blonde that it blurs together with the light.

Mama is in the other picture, a serious expression on her face and a few months pregnant. She's sitting on the edge of the bed in her bedroom at Grandma's house, the bedroom that later became my bedroom. Her face is puffy and her eyes are different sizes. A tiny white sweater resting on her knee.

It's as though she's trying to tell me something. That's what the look in her eyes says, and her lips are bending around a word. What is she thinking about?

ELÍN, MISC.

A jewelry box made of wood with painted-on bluebells and full of trinkets. Clip-on earrings made of plastic, a tarnished locket and knotted chains. A water-filled ball wearing my hair. Brown, dense, bristly. A leather pouch I've never seen before. A rusty harmonica. A piece of obsidian the size of a fist. A key. A tin box filled with my collection of decorative paper napkins. Moisture had gotten into the box and the napkins are moldy. A clay head. I'd tacked glass beads where the eyes should have been. A broken statuette of a poodle. The leather pouch is dry and yellow, and it crosses my mind that it's an ancient, dried-up scrotum. It cracks at my touch, disintegrates.

ELÍN, PAPERS

My diaries and a sheaf of papers. The paper I wrote on was thin, like baking paper, had become fragile over time. Moisture has come into contact with the ink and some of the words are now unreadable. The first story in the sheaf is about elves. I was fourteen years old when

I wrote it, and it ends with the main character waking up—it had all been a dream.

I remember that when I showed it to Grandma, she said that's how all stories ended, and I didn't understand what she meant, thought she was saying that my story was unoriginal. But when I think about it now, I understand exactly what she meant.

The skies are pale gray and there aren't many people out on this Wednesday morning. I'm walking down Bankastræti, but then all of a sudden, I come to a halt. This automatic movement, feet lifting in turn and easing me slowly down Bankastræti, isn't working anymore. The reflects . . . or what's the word? Doesn't work. People are walking toward me, looking searchingly at my face.

Everything changes. In an instant, and I don't know why. Words leave me, their context becomes unclear. Their definitions lose their authority. And then, my feet start moving again. Walk with me. Where am I going? To the post office, was that it? Was I going to mail a letter? Where was I mailing a letter to? To whom had I written what?

I remember as soon as I enter the post office. I take the slip triumphantly out of my bag and walk to the girl at the counter.

You have to take a number, she says, and I hold the slip out to her.

No, a number, she says and waves in the direction of something by the entrance.

I have a number, I say, and the girl sighs. Someone calls out that it's okay. I look around, see a bearded man holding a little child. He smiles at me and I smile back. The girl gets my delivery. It's a science magazine that I'm subscribed to. I remember now.

On the bus on the way home, I find a translation of a poetry collection by Ted Hughes in my handbag and gasp. I'd forgotten the library. The bus is almost all the way home, but I get to my feet all the same, intend to turn around somehow, but I quickly realize it's too late.

Are you okay? asks the woman sitting next to me.

The bookmobile, I say, and I don't know what I mean; I can hear how peculiar it sounds, want to explain, but I can't. The bus stops, and I recognize my stop, hurry out.

The bookmobile? I mutter to myself. Where did that come from? I walk straight home and I'm relieved when I close the front door behind me. Back in a safe harbor.

> What am I? Nosing here, turning leaves over
> Following a faint stain on the air to the river's edge
> I enter water. Who am I to split
> The glassy grain of water looking upward I see the bed
> Of the river above me upside down very clear

. . . I think, but where do these lines come from and why? My plants have been dying one after the other. First the big ficus in the television room, then the dragon lily in the living room, after that, the tomato plant in the kitchen. I don't know what I should do with them, don't feel right putting them in the trash, can't bring myself to fling them out into the garden, where they'll just wither away, slowly and steadily in their pots, then hopefully turn into soil in the end. How long would that take?

I look for my journal but don't find it right away. What else was I looking for?

I look out the window and see the redwings. They're drunk on fermented berries and unafraid of the cat that I notice now, too. It's lying under the rustling hedge, its eyes like saucers in its mesmerized face.

Of course, you don't talk about animals' faces, rather use special words like *snout* or *muzzle* to describe what is none other than a face. Animals have more of a face than people do, I think. Faces that are so unfamiliar you can hardly make out their distinctive features. Little die-cast masks.

People have wind in their faces, storms in their faces, have calm in their faces, have lies in their faces. A whole china service in their faces. A thousand-cup china service with a bird motif produced by some Danish company. The light blue base coat cracked.

Animals eat. People feed.

Animals drink. People lap.

Animals pass away. People are killed.

The girl in the attic apartment owns that cat. I've asked her numerous times to put a bell on it. The girl promises to do it but still never does. She's kind to me. Looks in on me sometimes and asks how my hip is doing when we cross paths in the laundry room.

When she first moved in, we sometimes sat and had a coffee together. The girl is a single mother and although she never goes into the details, I can make out from her words that the children's father isn't really in the picture.

Her name is Lena, or Jelena. Or maybe Helena. Something with an E. Ellen? Her cat gets into position, waggles its bottom side to side, and pounces at the redwing where it's lying drunk on its back in a pile of russet leaves. I knock on the windowpane, startle the cat a little, and it looks up but still doesn't let me distract him.

Damn top hat, I say and know I mean something else. I pull the curtain closed so I won't see the cat's attack.

I had these curtains made for me, but now I don't remember where or how come. I know that there's a story behind the curtains, a trip to Turkey or Portugal. The curtains are yellow and patterned and befitting of a palace. There's some story behind them. There was also a story behind the person who made them.

What was I looking for again? My journal. I'm going to write down something that occurred to me, some words I'm not sure are mine or if they're from something I read.

There are pots with dirt in the kitchen window. Nothing growing there anymore but I catch sight of something that's hanging down from the chain that's holding up the pot. Something that casts out in every direction, small and bushy. I perch on my tiptoes and pinch it between two fingers.

It's a little plant I've never seen before. The leaves are bright green and delicate, they seem to grow out from the middle, which is one big tangle. I consider this phenomenon from all angles, but don't see a beginning or end anywhere. I put the plant on the dirt in the pot and forget it immediately.

The girl is in the laundry room when I go to get the wash. The washing machine is empty.

How's the hip? asks the girl, and I say it's better.

The boys are at their grandma's, says the girl and then suggests we have a glass of red wine together. After all, it's Saturday night she says, but I say I don't have any red wine. I go back into my apartment to get the wash but find my journal on the telephone table.

Tillandsia, I write.

The girl knocks on my door. She's wearing a knit tunic, and there's a wooden bead necklace around her neck. Her hair is crimped, like it's been in a tight braid. She's holding a bottle and lifts it a little. I can clearly see that she's been crying.

Ellen, Edda, Hedda, Helga, Hekla, Heckle, Speckle, Hera, Hildur, Hidden, Kitten?

She sits at my kitchen table and peers at the little yellow notes on the wall.

Are you working on something? she asks, and I shrug.

I'm not wrippling anymore, I say. Wratting, wrotting, ritting. I give up, make a face.

Did you go to the doctor? asks the girl, getting up and finding glasses in the cupboard. She pours us wine, acts like she lives in my apartment.

I don't drink! I remember suddenly, and the girl jumps. She offers to put on a pot of coffee or make some tea, but I don't need anything. There are magnets and photographs on my refrigerator. The girl points at one and asks if that's me, there with a group of friends at the Piazza del Popolo. I look at the picture and see a few women striking a pose in front of a water fountain on a sunny day. They're lightly dressed for summer and smiling with big jewelry and big hairdos and the breeze rippling around their heads.

I have been so many women, I mumble, and the girl laughs unnecessarily loud.

Tell me about it, she says and asks if she can have a smoke out the window.

Behind the television, tangled in the cords, there's another plant. A little bit bigger than the previous one, its leaves longer and thicker. I free it and hold it in my palm. It weighs less than nothing.

The phone rings. It's the receptionist at the doctor's office, reminding me of the appointment I booked for later that day.

Are there plants that grow out of themselves? I ask the receptionist.

You mean like weeds? he asks.

No, no roots, just these leaves that grow out from the middle.

I don't know enough about gardening . . .

It's an inside plant; I found it behind the television.

Hmmm . . . says the receptionist, and I hang up.

I pace back and forth around the apartment for a long time with the plant in my hands and don't know what I should do. So I find a pot in the living room that has nothing but dirt in it. I put the plant on the dirt.

The book is still in my pocket. I come across it when I'm looking for my journal one morning, and when I see it, I let out a low cry.

It's very overdue, I think and am going to check but then no matter how long I stare at the calendar, I can't figure out what day it is. I'm not even sure what month it is. There's a naked tree out in the garden and under it, a blackish-brown pile of leaves.

Late fall, I think and look in the back of the library book but every time that I look away from the date I forget it and decide to go to the library without delay.

The book that I need to return is a recent translation of a poetry collection by Ted Hughes. I don't remember if I read it. *When*, I say quietly, and am startled when I hear my own voice.

I set off with the book in my handbag. I am going to return it to the library downtown. The bus stop seems to have been moved a ways off, and I decide to walk. It won't take more than half an hour and the weather is good. The buds on the trees are opening like little green hands.

What am I? Nosing here. Turning leaves over, following a faint stain on the air to the river's edge, I suddenly think and then wonder why I don't go out more often. You'd think that many decades had passed since I last went out for a walk. Everything has changed so much. Now there are thoroughfares where there used to be walking paths, and they've put up a shopping center where there used to be a public park.

I don't know how long I've been walking when I realize that I'm lost. There's no one around. Just the cars rumbling past. Then finally, I see someone walking toward me along the road—it's a boy, probably no more than ten years old. He's pulling something behind him in a wagon and when he gets all the way up to me, I see that he's all covered in ink.

Excuse me, I say, and the boy stops, his bright blue eyes gazing at me from his grimy face.

Excuse me, but I want to go downtown, I say, and the boy tells me to turn around.

It could take a long time, though, he says. Maybe two hours on foot.

What time is it? I ask then, and he says he doesn't have a clock but that it's probably around six in the morning. All of a sudden, the traffic falls silent. I say goodbye to the boy and turn around. I can hear the traffic again, and I walk the same way back. Always in the direction of the sun, I think.

In the direction of the sun, in the direction of the sun, in the direction of the sun. I have to say the sentence over and over so I don't forget it. I look up at the sky and see the sun out in front of me. In the direction of the sun, in the direction of the sun, in the direction of the sun. But why do I need to go in the direction of the sun? What is there?

My words become useless right as their context vanishes, a heap of garbage. There's the public park and there's a glowing orb and there's my bus stop and there's the orb and it gets closer to me and gets bigger and ignites everything and everything turns orange red and I get hot.

I enter water, I think, *who am I to split the glassy grain of water looking upward I see the bed of the river above me upside down very clear.*

Where are these words coming from? I don't remember, but they continue to turn over in my head accompanied by a cadence and voice. A deep voice that breaks into heaving sobs and howls between words.

> *What am I doing here in mid-air? Why do I find*
> *this frog so interesting as I inspect its most secret*
> *interior and make it my own? Do these weeds*
> *know me and name me to each other have they*
> *seen me before do I fit in their world? I seem*
> *separate from the ground and not rooted but dropped*
> *out of nothing casually I've no threads*
> *fastening me to anything I can go anywhere*
> *I seem to have been given the freedom*
> *of this place what am I then? And picking*
> *bits of bark off this rotten stump gives me*
> *no pleasure and it's no use so why do I do it*
> *me and doing that have coincided very queerly*
> *But what shall I be called am I the first*
> *have I an owner what shape am I what*
> *shape am I am I huge if I go*
> *to the end on this way past these trees and past these trees*

till I get tired that's touching one wall of me
for the moment if I sit still how everything
stops to watch me I suppose I am the exact centre
but there's all this what is it roots
roots roots roots and here's the water
again very queer but I'll go on looking

I'm home again and can't find my journal. Was that something I composed or something I read or something I'm always about to write? I don't know, and I don't find my journal, and the yellow notes are long gone. I don't know where to get more.

I walk around the apartment and turn everything upside down, looking, my belongings seem unbeatable, laughing at me, scoffing at my thoughts. I take a vase off the shelf. A small, handmade porcelain vase. I look at it and know there is a story behind it. Maybe something related to my grandma, but that's nothing but conjecture.

These things don't touch me anymore, and I take the vase and throw it at the wall. I feel good for a little while. As I collect the shards and sift through them, I run my fingers along the broken edges.

Gently.

The man's voice has quieted. The cries live on for a while in the air, but now I hear someone rattling at the door and a key is turned in the lock.

Halló? I hear a familiar woman's voice say, and I also hear a child's voice. The child's voice sounds like a silver bell.

Elín? calls the woman, and I'm going to answer but there's something blocking my throat. Then she's standing there in the hall, windswept and wholesome, and there's a child with her who babbles unremittingly.

Elín, dear? she says and bends over me.

Why are you lying on the floor, Elín, dear, she says. Did you not hear the phone?

The woman's eyes are filled with tears, and I am going to answer but I can't. I want to tell her about all the strange things that have been happening but in my throat, where before a river ran, there is now a dam. The words collect in a wellspring inside me and suddenly, I see the child.

The child holds on tight to the woman, stands there on unsteady feet. We are silent and look into each other's eyes, over a glassy grain, and we meet each other in the middle.

Hi, says the child, without opening his mouth:

Hi, my old friend, it's so good to see you again. I missed you, but can see now that was unnecessary. Hi, old friend. Hi.

Like silver bells.

ABOUT THE AUTHOR

Photo © 2019 Forlagid

Kristín Eiríksdóttir is an award-winning novelist, short story writer, poet, and playwright from Reykjavík, Iceland. Her original edition of *A Fist or a Heart* won the Icelandic Literary Prize 2017 as well as the Icelandic Women's Literature Prize 2018, and was nominated for the Nordic Council Literature Prize 2019. The novel took second place for the Icelandic Booksellers' Prize and was selected as one of the best novels of 2017 by the Icelandic National Broadcasting Service. Eiríksdóttir has published seven books and had three plays staged. Her short fiction has appeared in *Best European Fiction 2011*. *A Fist or a Heart* is her first novel to be translated into English.

ABOUT THE TRANSLATOR

Photo © 2018 Caitlyn Morrissey

Larissa Kyzer is a writer and translator. She holds an MS in library and information science and a BA in comparative literature. In 2012, she received a Fulbright grant to Iceland, where she lived for five years and earned an MA in translation studies. Her published translations have been varied and include novels, children's books and chapter books for young readers, short stories, poetry, essays, and nonfiction. Kyzer is a board member of Ós, an Iceland-based international and literary collective, and is a member of the American Literary Translators Association and PEN America. She lives in Brooklyn, New York.